Mokita

Mokita

John Philipose

ZORBA BOOKS

ZORBA BOOKS

Published by Zorba Books, December 2023

Website: www.zorbabooks.com
Email: info@zorbabooks.com
Title: Mokita
Author Name: John Philipose
Copyright ©: John Philipose

Printbook ISBN: 978-93-95217-88-0
Ebook ISBN: 978-93-95217-84-2

All rights reserved. No part of this book may be reproduced or transmitted in any form or by any means, electronic or mechanical, except by a reviewer who may quote brief passages, with attribution, in a review to be printed in a magazine, newspaper, or on the Web—without permission in writing from the copyright owner.
The publisher under the guidance and direction of the author has published the contents in this book, and the publisher takes no responsibility for the contents, its accuracy, completeness, any inconsistencies, or the statements made. The contents of the book do not reflect the opinion of the publisher or the editor. The publisher and editor shall not be liable for any errors, omissions, or the reliability of the contents of the book.
Any perceived slight against any person/s, place or organization is purely unintentional.

Zorba Books Pvt. Ltd. (opc)
Sushant Arcade,
Next to Courtyard Marriot,
Sushant Lok 1, Gurgaon – 122009, India

Printed by Manipal Technologies Limited
A1 & A2 Shivalli Industrial Area Manipal Udupi, Karnataka - 576104

Dedicated

Rose Philipose my beloved wife,
my children and family

Contents

Acknowledgement .... *ix*
Author's Note .... *xi*
Foreword .... *xiii*
Preface .... *xv*

Chapter 1 1
Chapter 2 16
Chapter 3 29
Chapter 4 38
Chapter 5 50
Chapter 6 65
Chapter 7 83
Chapter 8 91
Chapter 9 100
Chapter 10 112
Chapter 11 127
Chapter 12 142
Chapter 13 155
Chapter 14 176

Acknowledgement

I would like to express my heartfelt gratitude to Irene Gupta for sparing her time and effort in editing my book. She had exceptional patience and her positive criticism greatly appreciated.

My sincere thanks to Tenslin Augustine for designing the cover and his constant support from the beginning till day for the successful completion of the book.

I also express gratitude to J. K.Varghese (Sunny) for assisting in the production of the book.

Girish Varghese and Dominic Joseph were always there.

Mr. R. Prassanan:	Resident Editor. Malayala Manorama & The Week for sparing his valuable time for writing the foreword deserves my special appreciation and gratitude.
Alex Joseph:	Advocate on Record, Supreme Court of India Greatly obliged to him for taking time to write an analytical study about the characters of book.

Author's Note

The novel is entirely a work of fiction. The names, characters, and incidents portrayed in it are the product of author's imagination. Any resemblance of any characters to any person, dead or alive, events or location is entirely coincidental.

Foreword

The novel Mokita mentions or talks about more than 45 characters. Though the novel as an artistic work is not running into more than 200 pages, how it remains as a distinct and different work is that each character has his own background and story to narrate. So, it fulfills one of the features of a legendary artistic work. The novel also exposes the foul – play and dirty tactics prevailing in the Art world to its readers and such a microscopic realistic revelation rarely happens in a literary work. More than a happy ending on account of untold reunion of a mother and her abandoned child, the author has tried his level best to convey several touching messages from his observations in life to his readers. In fact, the title 'Mokita' itself is a classic example of the same i.e. 'truth - everybody knows but no one wants to talk about'. Later I learned from my personal interaction with the author that his exposure, among the art fraternity was valuable help to accomplish to write this novel. The author being an artist himself used them as colors to mix up to give a unique shade and thus the novel 'Mokita' is born.

— **Alex Joseph**
Advocate on record
Supreme Court

Preface

I am a poor scribe with no touch of art, either in my heart or in my mind. I knew John Philipose only as one of India's finest musicologists; museums for me were and still are places where objects from the bygone ages are displayed.

So when John Philipose approached me with a request to write a Preface to his book which he said dealt with the world of art, I had two thoughts in my mind. One, this is not the guy who should be writing books on art; he should be writing about artifacts. Two, I am not the guy to write prefaces to this book; I should be writing, if at all, prefaces to books that dealt with things less sublime.

Then he made two confessions. One, that he himself is an artist. I was elated. Two, this book is less about art and more about frauds in the world of art. The criminal mind in me was further elated. Now he was talking! Without me realizing it, I said yes.

Indeed, I had read up a little on frauds in the world of art and artifacts a few months earlier when my home state of Kerala was shocked, rocked and amused by the incredible adventures of a fraudster. The guy had made a few big worthies of India's most literate state believe that he had in his possession the scepter carried by Moses, the clay pot in which Ma Yasoda of Gokul had secreted her butter stock away from the prankster Krishna's reach, and even the more recent throne on which Tiger Tipu of Mysore sat. Not only had this guy sold those stories to several gullible millionaires, but also made them buy a few of his artifacts and even invest in his business.

Let me confess, I got tickled reading the adventures of this Natwarlal of Kerala. Soon I collected a few books on fraudsters, read them up. All my little reading about the world of art frauds didn't shock me. Rather, they amused me. As I read how Mona Lisa was stolen, copied and the copies sold as original, how great institutions like the Smithsonian had been duped, I began to develop some respect and regard for these so-called fraudsters. After all, they themselves are talented artists in their own right; how else could they make copies that looked often more original than the original? The owed our respect and regards as artists in their own right.

I also discovered one thing - that there is no shame attached to art fraud. I read somewhere that even Michaelangelo had sculpted an "ancient" Greek statue and sold it to a gullible bishop.

In this book, Philipose tells us the stories of such smart Alecs thorough the main narrative which is the story of an art teacher who was born an orphan. He gets to ghost-paint for his school principal, a socialite who helps him feather his nest. The story is not about any crime being committed or caught; for there is no sense of sin, guilt or crime. Rather the story is is about the pains and pangs of conscience felt by the young art teacher now and then.

The theme of art frauds comes out as asides in the narration of the life story of the protagonist. He has a friend, guide and mentor who knows all the good and bad things in the world of art and art business, and from his small talk with other characters in the book we learn about the fraudulent activities.

It is those asides that come through the narration that makes this book interesting. My best wishes.

– R. Prassanan
Resident Editor
Malayala Manorama & The Week
New Delhi

Chapter 1

It was a balmy evening. The sprawling lawns of the India International Centre were a happy venue, as many among Delhi's well-heeled gentry had gathered to celebrate the betrothal of the capital's rising Bharatnatyam star Revathy Chinappa to one of the blue-eyed boys of the incumbent regime. Soft strains of sitar mingled with laughter and the clink of glasses. Guests sat around the lawn in groups of six or seven, sipping their aperitifs, as the hosts moved from table to table to chitchat with the invitees. Brigadier Rajesh Chopra and his wife, Seema Chopra, were seated with their circle of friends. The group, mostly former defence personnel and bureaucrats and their better halves, were engaged in discussing the prospects of their own offspring, as is often the case when elderly couples with marriageable children gather at such occasions.

"What did you gain from your twenty-five years of service? The children are doing well because they opted to be in the Army. They got selected because of their merit." These kinds of barbs were nothing new to the good Brigadier. This was not the first time that Seema had decided to launch a frontal attack on him in public.

"Indeed, my wife is very unfortunate that she was unable to obtain a Param Vir Chakra from the President of India. You would have received the award, followed by some land and a licence for a gas station and a petrol pump. Really, you are unlucky, my dear." Brigadier Rajesh replied sarcastically. "Please stop this nonsense" A visibly upset Seema hissed.

There are two main reasons for these periodic outbursts. One: to prove among friends that the Chopras are honest; and second: most of the achievements, the friends must realise, come from Seems's earnings as Principal of Delhi International School (DIS).

2 Mokita

It is not necessary that every successful family have posthumous awards to avail themselves of the opportunity. In financial stakes, Brig. Chopra was an exception. A straight-forward and honest officer, he did not seize many opportunities. During his service, he could have earned more through unfair means. His wife's biggest grouse was that they had to make do with an Army housing apartment.

Seema dreamed of purchasing a farmhouse in Chattarpur like her friends, most of whom have large flower gardens and space for keeping more dogs and pets. But in an apartment, there is limited space, and sometimes they have heated arguments about the subject. But most importantly, it was a status symbol. "Seema, please be reasonable; your school is built on 5 acres of land. You have the largest lawns compared to any public school in Delhi," Rajesh consoled her. "Please, Rajesh, don't ridicule; sometimes be realistic." Seema loses her cool. He falls silent. Her comments are always accepted as a superior's order. Once an Army man, always an Army man.

Seema had numerous possibilities after graduating to wed an IAS, IFS, or IRS officer, but she decided against it after seeing a Republic Day parade with her father, Sandeep Arora, a government employee from the Rajasthan cadre. To view the parade, her father used to get a VIP pass. She saw the President honour handsome, well-built military men with shiny medals. She had said, "What a majestic walk!" as they came to receive the trophies. There and then, she made up her mind: "Dad, if I marry, I will only wed an Army Officer."

"Think it over; don't regret it later; there is still plenty of time." When he responded, her father was quite serious.

"No, Dad. I'm only getting married to an Army officer." The young Seema was emphatic and uncompromising.

When Paulo Coelho said, "Once you dream, the whole world comes behind you to fulfil the dream," she dreamed and took him at his word.

Her childhood, though happy, was hopelessly monotonous and drab. Much like the three-bedroom government quarter that her father was allotted in Rama Krishna Puram, her dad's regular office routine included her mother preparing the typical lunch of *roti* and *sabzi* and packing her father's tiffin carrier. In fifteen years, the tiffin carrier had not been changed. He wore the same blue blazer and high-neck sweater every winter. A simple, honest man who is not very ambitious. Mummy was always content, never made any demands, was very studious, and only cared that her two children got well educated. The only luxury they enjoyed was the annual holiday they could avail themselves of under the Leave Travel Concession [LTC], during which they visited many tourist sites in India. It was the one exciting thing she could describe to her friends.

Her brother joined an information technology company, married a Kannadiga woman in the same line of work, and decided to settle in Bangalore. Seema and her brother exchanged greetings on all festivals and occasions. In the last three decades, she never missed sending him the 'rakhi',' and he found time to send her gifts to celebrate their bond.

Back home, as the Chopras sat in companionable silence, the evening's acrimonious outbursts drowned in the glasses of Scotch, Seema's classmate from school, Sunita Goyal, called to invite her to an upcoming art show. Sunita, one of her classmates, had cracked the proverbial glass ceiling and made her presence felt in the male-dominated Revenue Department. And alongwith it had come the unspoken perks like concessions even at top-star hotels, which Seema was privy to when the two classmates and their kitty group met for lunch. But more importantly, she was an acclaimed artist today who was being showered with praise by art critics. Her shows were all successful, and most of her works sold out on the inaugural day itself.

Though she was happy with Sunita's success, it baffled her as well. In school, Sunita was anything but an artist. In fact, she used to seek Seema's assistance in drawing the most basic diagrams for biology class. She had shown no aptitude for drawing or art. Then how did she become a celebrated artist overnight? Always managing to be in the 'Page 3' columns of some national daily. How did she manage her very taxing and responsible job and also find time to paint? Where and when did she learn painting? She claimed she was self-taught. Art critics write very highly of her, calling her 'a genius'.

Even though she was very close to Sunita, did she ever invite her to visit her studio? Maybe artists never want anyone to visit their workspace. Though their girly gossip covered everything under the sun, Sunita hardly ever said anything about her painting. "Rajesh, what I don't understand is how the media features her on Page 3. There is not a single senior artist who has not kissed her cheek. Don't you think this is a rather cheesy affair?" Seema's expression of surprise was laced with a hint of jealousy. "What is your problem? You too were in the news with your annual function awards with cabinet ministers and all," the Brigadier casually replied.

"Please don't be silly! Who would have known me if they hadn't printed my name, DIS Principal Seema Chopra? She expresses her dissatisfaction. She was really dissatisfied with the write-ups. "I am heading a kitty party group of twenty-five rich, affluent, and influential ladies of the city. Over and above that, I am the Principal of a nationally reputed school. But does it even matter?" she said.

"Who cares about all these? Your job as a Principal is important. See how many young minds you are shaping?"

"I do care. I want to be rich and affluent. I too want to be famous; otherwise, there is no fun in this kind of life. I have just 3 years of my service left. Dear man, who the hell is going to recognise us tomorrow if we do not build up our base now?"

"Seema, you know what time it is now? Nearly 11 p.m. Let us go to sleep. Please, dear, our whole life is ahead; we can discuss this tomorrow". Rajesh pleaded.

Once in bed, she took out an extra pillow whenever she felt disturbed. She lay on her stomach and hoped to fall asleep, resting her head on her left arm while bending her left leg. There are many ways to find fulfilment in life, and every individual has his own priorities. One can be satisfied with what one has. But Seema always wanted to be the exception, wherever she was—Principal, kitty party leader. There was enough money to live well. She earned a fat salary, her husband had a good pension, and her children were both in the Army. What else could she ask for? In school, she always had a special say, and trustees and board members always stood with her for improvement or expansion, the appointment of new faculty, or anything related to the school. But this was definitely not enough for her. "I have to do something," she murmured.

"Seema, sleep." Rajesh's hand was on her shoulder, massaging her neck. Usually she relaxed and slept, but today her mind was not allowing her to rest. Her art department had two full-time teachers, but she hardly ever recognised their contributions. She gave priority to sports and games. Many awards added to the popularity of the school. Considering the present scenario in the country's Art Market, especially for paintings by contemporary painters, it is possible to win fame and make big money. If one were to take Sunita's example, with popularity and media coverage, one can hopefully become famous overnight.

And age was not a factor. After all, M.F. Hussain was painting at the age of 90. I am only 55, just half his age. Of course, she is doing a wonderful job, holding a good position, being well respected, and having only three years to retire. The rules of the school provide no scope for an extension, howsoever efficient the Principal may be.

If something is not worked out now, when? A big question. She tossed and turned, but sleep evaded her. The air conditioner's hum and Rajesh's soft snores broke the stillness of the room. She didn't know how long she lay there, toying with various ideas and discarding them one by one. It must have been well past midnight when the answer to her problems came to her in a flash. She jumped and sat up in bed. Her brow was beaded with perspiration. The art teachers in her school are Ashok Daniel and Richa Chadha! She could seek their help. The solution had been staring her in the face all this time, but she never recognised it.

The school always focussed on sports, elocution, and theatre. Therefore, the art department inadvertently came out as drab and colourless. The fault lay with her. She ought to have taken more initiative to enhance the art department and inspire teachers, given her position of authority. Now, if she moves too fast, there is a possibility of suspicion. Her plan was pretty easy: she would start an art workshop and provide orientation for all teachers who wanted to join the class for two hours a day, three days a week. No fees will be charged by the staff. Art teachers would conduct the workshop. Considering art awareness in the present scenario, there would be no suspicion. She would make sure all teachers joined the workshop. In the process, she too will brush up on her skills and step into the art world. And hopefully, she will succeed like Sunita.

Having worked out her plan, she finally slept. The maid came and knocked on the door to serve the coffee. Seema's eyes opened for a new sunrise, a new chapter in her life. Rajesh had already left for jogging. She must get ready and rush to school; there are many things to be worked out. She had to be active in the school, with 1,800-odd students from 4 years to 16 and 120 staff working.

On reaching school, Seema felt like a little girl, almost dying of excitement. Wanting to rush through the morning tasks at school and immediately call the art teacher. She had to tell herself to calm down. It was only after the 8 a.m. morning assembly that she sent a handwritten note to Ashok Daniel.

When the peon came with the Principal's note summoning him, Daniel was a little puzzled. He could hardly remember any occasion in the three years of his career when the Principal had called him to her cabin.

'Dear Mr. Daniel, you are free to meet me any time after your class. Prepare a note on how to improve your department and requirements. I have to prepare a project report for discussion with the Board. Come prepared and meet me soon as the class is over'.

Daniel stood looking at the note. Surprised and puzzled. She never recognised his existence after his appointment almost 3 years ago. Well, she might have realised that art and artists have a market in today's world. He had to be ready and prepared in three hours. Should he not be discussing this development with his colleague, Richa Chadha? She too was part of the art department as the sculpture teacher. But the Principal had nowhere mentioned that he should discuss with his colleague or bring her along for the meeting. So he decided to remain silent until his meeting with the Principal was over.

He went to the staff washroom with his small hand towel, which he always carried in his bag. He washed his hands to make sure there was no colour under the nails and rubbed them dry. He looked at himself in the mirror. At 5' 10," he was tall by Indian standards. Olive skinned, with a well-groomed beard, broad shoulders under a crisp blue shirt, and well-ironed grey trousers. Athletic built the kind one would associate with a volleyball player or a swimmer. Would anyone looking at him think he is an artist? No, he never carried a *jhola*, nor was he seen in sandals or *chappals* at work, and neither was he caught with a cigarette or a *beedi*, the fashionable smoke that most of his college mates used to indulge in. Only his eyes looked a tad puffy.

Yes, he was tired. He had been painting late into the night for an exhibition for his friend Surya's client. In the last couple of weeks, most nights were spent in the studio trying to complete this commercial assignment. He reminded himself that after meeting the Principal, he had to head straight for Triveni Art Gallery for Sunita Goyal's solo show. But before that, it must be ensured that he has everything ready, especially the written report. He is going to meet the Principal in her cabin, a rare opportunity. He was carrying a list of items the department needed: one more assistant, six more aisles, and more art materials, plus a list of programmes to be planned for exhibitions to be conducted quarterly for student work in the school meeting hall. Invite VIPs or some influential parents of the students as the chief guests. But foremost, he must meet her with a smile and wish her well. He could not afford to look nervous.

Oh no, as she has called him, he must not rush her. She has to speak her mind. Daniel has to be the listener, but he must be prepared to answer all queries. In his mind, he checked off all the boxes and headed for the meeting.

Unlike his previous experiences, the peon accompanied him to the door of the Principal's cabin and opened it for him. The peon understood the pulse of his boss, or he might have read the note she sent.

As scheduled, the meeting was over and very cordial. He did not have to make the customary three rounds of the veranda before he was allowed in. She was never free because of PTA, teachers, guests, and VIPs; the peon is the actual secretary; without his wish, no entry was allowed.

Madame Principal was also very warm. No frown, but instead an unusually big smile. She requested that he sit on the visitor's sofa instead of the chair facing the desk. She crossed over and sat across from him. The meeting had an informal air to it; nothing seemed official. He sat down like an obedient child and addressed her,

"Good afternoon, Ma'am".

"Yes, good afternoon, Daniel. I must mention that you are the only staff member who has visited my cabin not more than three or four times since you joined." There was a great warmth in her voice.

"Yes, Ma'am," Daniel replied.

"It means you have nothing to complain about or did not want to trouble me." She seemed to be in a very jovial mood.

"Sorry, Ma'am. You were always busy; your cabin always had visitors. Many times, Rawat denied me entry, saying you were in a meeting. But that's okay," he blurted out the truth.

She merely smiled and moved straight into the subject matter of the meeting. She detailed how to start the workshop, how to invite all teachers who are interested in art, prepare the list of materials, and all the other requirements. She requested that he accord high priority to these tasks, as this project had been very much on her mind for the last six months. Daniel left the office in a hurry, intending to quickly do all the homework she had assigned to him.

After Daniel left, Seema thought through her plan again. She had barely 3 years left before retirement, out of which at least one year would go into practice before she could be rated as a reasonably good artist. She realised it would be difficult to reach anywhere at this time. There was an urgent need to speed up the process, so she decided to invite Daniel to her home. Also, the teachers should not feel like Madam Principal is a greenhorn when the workshop begins. She was feeling restless and keen to find out how and where to start, so there was nothing wrong with taking his input. She again sent a note to him.

"Tomorrow being a holiday, join me for breakfast, initialled S.C." The stapled, folded paper took Daniel hardly any time to open. He read it and murmured to himself, "a God-given opportunity". He felt as if his wife Sarah's prayers had been heard. Once Seema Ma'am was familiar with him, it would be the right time to approach her to sanction a loan from the school so that they could book an apartment.

Daniel reached the Principal's residence at the stipulated time, carrying with him all the initial materials required to start art training.

After breakfast, Seema asked very casually, "Do you always carry a sketchbook and materials?"

"Not always. Sometimes on holidays, I go to monument sites and parks. Today, it is different. Sincerely, I felt I could offer to come and help you at home. A Principal studying with junior teachers at school does not look fair." He said it with childlike candour.

Could he read her mind? Though she loved the idea, there was surprise on her face.

"For me, I am always a student and have the right attitude for learning. We are seekers and should not feel embarrassed. Anyway, you know my problem. I won't be able to devote enough time to the workshop. But of course, my colleagues should not feel that I am not part of it. I will come on casual visits to the workshop to keep their spirits high."

"Ma'am, you come for a little time. After school, I go to my studio. Whenever you have time, just send a message. I will come home and teach you."

This is exactly what Seema had planned. This youngster understands the need of the hour; he deserves better treatment in school—a thought that never occurred to her before. Daniel realised he would have to divide the after-school working hours between the art workshop, commercial work, and Seemaji. As he left her house, he decided that however he might divide his time, working for Seema Ma'am would be his first priority. Seema decided that no kitty member should know that she has started attending art class and has a school tutor at home. She was full of enthusiasm, much like a college girl. The artist in her will soon be reborn and blossom. When the Brigadier learned of this, he was also happy. His wife's preoccupation would leave him free to enjoy golf.

Daniel demanded nothing, even after six months of working together. He would sit and sketch in a small room converted to a studio, which was previously the children's study. Even without telling her, he brought his art supplies one day, along with two small canvases and acrylic colours.

"I was about to ask you when I could work on canvas." Seema was so anxious, like a child wanting to see her first work on canvas.

"Ma'am, it doesn't need any time or day; just your will and time. It will always come to you, and you have to be like a thief to rob," Daniel said with sincerity.

That was a challenge; she would have to start. Daniel drew a large circle on the small canvas, just the outline, and requested that she fill in the colours. She felt it was an auspicious start. They started together to sketch the figure of 'Ganesha'," and it took almost three hours. The time passed without any feelings of boredom or tiredness.

"Daniel, you have to go far. It's already 8.30 Brigadier Sahab comes at 10.30. He may not join me for dinner. Why don't you have dinner with me? I want to celebrate this moment of happiness and make it memorable. I used acrylic colours for the first time. And, if you don't mind my asking, what should I do for you? You have no idea how grateful I am."

This was the moment he had been waiting for.

"Ma'am, I would be grateful if the school gave me an advance to buy a one-room flat near Kalkaji Extension. It is not too far from Sangam Vihar, where I stay now. What to do? There is no other option," Daniel said.

"I can arrange for a small apartment to stay in; no rent is required. We bought one EWS flat for our driver to stay in, but now we have changed our mind," Seema said.

"Thank you, Ma'am, but I've already paid an advance to a private builder. My wife has been in Bangalore since we married 18 months ago. There is a lot of pressure from the orphanage managed by a convent where she is sheltered to take her away. As soon as the house is ready, I will bring her to Delhi. If I can be frank with you, Ma'am, I'd like to say something". His throat became dry. His mind said, 'Be strong; shoot, shoot, say'.

"Daniel, be open and frank; you can tell me what is on your mind," she said.

"Ma'am, we are a group of four artists from the same college: Amal, Ranjan, and, of course, Surya; all are painters. All are struggling artists. None of them has a regular income to survive except me. All are doing painting, commissioned assignments, partly for housewives who have aspirations to be painters and to be in the limelight," he said in one breath.

"You mean the ladies buy the paintings?" Seema wanted to clear her doubts.

"No, Ma'am, they commission the work; we do the painting; they only sign and write their name on the back. Don't be surprised; we never disclose all this to anyone. I am disclosing this to you because I do not want to hide anything from you. In the last show at AIFACS, showing Sunita Madam's work, you were also there; all the work was ours. Ma'am, trust me, a good percentage of freelance, upcoming artists of the work in Delhi—paintings and sculptures—is done by people like us, except for the signature." He went on to explain that, much like ghost-writers he and his friends are hired to paint for celebrated artists or even newbies.

"Where would all these celebrities get time to work? They trust us as much as we do each other. On the inaugural day, we are never invited, just as the ghost writer will never be invited on the day of the book release. The next day, after seeing the newspaper and TV channel, we give feedback to the so-called artists who conduct the show." Daniel was now making so many revelations.

"You never have regrets?" she inquired.

"No, it is an assignment, commercial work. We do the job, and they pay with pleasure. Both parties are happy. They need paintings, and we want money to survive. Trust me, Ma'am, I never felt otherwise. It is a mindset. You hired me, I have to fulfil the commitment."

"If anyone comes to know?" Seema asked.

"Your doubt is genuine. Many celebrities can't walk or talk, but they are holding one-man shows, sponsored by big gallery houses. These are all very small happenings in the art market. We get paid a fee for our work.

"How did you like Megha Gupta's work on the Tantric theme?" At the last show, works ranging in price from Rs. 50,000 to Rs. 1.5 lakh sold out on the same day. We each received between Rs. 15,000 and Rs. 40,000; we have no regrets. We've heard she's going to open an art gallery." Daniel was in a good mood to discuss everything going on in the art world in and around Delhi.

While he was narrating, Seema sat in stunned silence.

"Ma'am, why are you so silent? I didn't mean to offend in any way. I was only trying to convince you how the so-called upcoming artists come into the limelight," Daniel said.

"No, no, Daniel, that's okay." In this school alone, I am completing eighteen years and have all the infrastructure. And even though you have been here for two years," Seema expressed her disappointment.

"No, Ma'am, it's almost three and a half years," Daniel corrected her. She was thinking about how much time and opportunity she had lost. Why did it never strike her before?

"Always in my speeches, while addressing students, I used to say opportunity never knocks twice; never wait for anybody. Anyway, you've never mentioned anything to me until now. You are so talented and skilled; why did you not come to me earlier?"

After a little silence, he replied, "Everyone says you're unfriendly and unapproachable. I was a bit scared."

"What do you think now?"

"There is a saying that appearances are deceptive."

"This seems true with both of us," Seema smiled.

"Yes, Ma'am, don't worry. I will compensate for the lost time. I will work overtime in my studio; you provide the required materials. Before our school closes for the annual holidays, you can have a solo show. Everyone will be surprised," Daniel said.

Seema gave a hearty laugh. "Solo show, whose work?"

"Please take it easy, Ma'am. I am with you; we will work together. Just give me a little time whenever you are free. Just SMS me," Daniel made the offer.

"My dear, please explain my role and contribution to the project."

"It is pretty easy; I have many contacts. We have a small group of artists. Before your solo show, you will participate in their group show for a small contribution of Rs. 5,000 to display two of your works. Just give your profile, biodata, and one photograph. I will paint, you just sign. This cannot be delayed because there are only eight months left for vacations," he explained.

"But, dear, what is my contribution?"

"I told you Rs. 5,000 for framing, material costs, etc. Please give at least twenty names of your intimate friends. In the future, they can be your buyers, and we will include them in our mailing list. If you can contribute another Rs. 5,000, you will get an additional 25 copies of the catalogue. Come a little early to the inauguration because someone from the media will be there. Bring friends. If we can arrange publicity, one of your paintings will be printed in Saturday's Delhi Times. Keep a small envelope with a visiting card and write up about yourself, one postcard-size photo of the painting, and a cash gift of Rs. 2,000 for the media rep, but it is up to you." Daniel explained the modus operandi in detail.

"You mean to say it's that simple?" Seema expressed her doubts.

"It is not, but with contacts and with the help of our fraternity, after two or three exhibitions, we will get coverage from some TV channel. Which group show would you like to participate in? I am in touch with four groups: Sudhir Kumar, Simran Bedi, Nitish Rai, and Anil Rathod. We can guarantee at least five shows. You will be in the limelight as a painter, another feather in your cap," Daniel said.

"Daniel, tell me sincerely, why are you doing all these things to help me out? You told me so many things that were not even in my wildest dreams. You took me to another world," Seema said, so excited.

"Well, you'll be the first person to hear me say I'm an orphan." My mother was from Kerala. I was raised in an orphanage of Mothers Of Charity till the age of five. Then I was in the Gabriel Brothers' orphanage. When I passed my Class 12 exam with honours, an unknown person gifted me this watch, which is on my wrist. I'm quite sure one of my parents sent it to me through my mentors. My mother, whoever she may be gave birth to me. That was the only mistake she made. If she isn't a saint, she must be; I adore her." Daniel's eyes welled up despite his best efforts to hide his emotions.

His revelations touched Seema's heart. She became very emotional, stood up, came forward, put her palm on his forehead, and said, "I never meant to hurt you."

"I am fine, Ma'am. You asked why I did not ask for anything from you. I don't know. Never had love from any siblings, parents, or grandparents. The orphanage run by the Gabriel Brothers is exclusively a male domain. When I meet a lady, I am nervous and lose self-confidence. Here with you, I feel like a child telling a story. Sorry, I don't know why I said all this," he said, keeping his eyes downcast.

"Don't worry, Daniel, you are now in my school; go peacefully. We will talk next time; today it's very late. We will plan and do everything as discussed. Again, thank you so much, Daniel."

"Ma'am, please. I am very grateful for this opportunity."

He felt they could build great trust in subsequent meetings when they said goodbye.

Seema held his hand while saying goodbye. She sensed from his soft palm that he was very sensitive, a young lad who lacked love and confidence. When he left, she felt a sort of loneliness. He was a very vibrant, energetic, and enthusiastic young man, full of ideas that needed to be explored. She went to bed that night with happy dreams of becoming an artist, a celebrity in the art world, and a resident of the capital, Delhi. Daniel had come into her life as a saviour.

Chapter 2

As Principal, Seema had to prepare notes for the management committee, initiate discussions to prioritize which departments called for attention and focus. Certainly, the art department needed a facelift and additional facilities. Convincing the Board should not be too difficult. She was after all a master at it. Even then questions were swarming in her head.

Could she trust this boy? Daniel was very positive and confident when he talked about the project. The question mark is over her own contribution: the time limit, school timing 7 am to 4 pm, weekly reviews with the management, PTA meetings, listening to teacher and staff grievances. How much time could she really devote? Can she pull it off? Or was she merely building castles in the air?

She consoled herself, at least she had started using colours and brush on canvas, the basics. Before she proceeded any further, must make sure what all is needed of her. How much effort must she make or will Daniel handle everything for her.

Daniel was very particular that she visit Sunita Goyal's exhibition to get a real feel of such artists. One thing was certain: she cannot ask Sunita as to who is assisting her. It would not only sound ridiculous but would sow the seeds of distrust as well. She could not afford to lose a long-cherished friend. Though they gossiped about everything under the sky but she never heard anything from Sunita about her paintings. 'Why did Sunita not even on one occasion mention she is taking help from outside? We discuss about everything: man to woman, perfumes to saris and undergarments. She may be thinking if I come to know, I will also get into the same field,' Seema reasoned.

She switched off the TV, raised her leg, rested it on the centre table top and leaned back on the sofa. She placed an extra cushion on the back to support her neck, told herself to relax and contemplate on all that she learnt from Daniel today.

It was like an episode right out of a TV serial – so unrealistic, fictitious and yet she realized it was true. She had heard of ghost-writing but what Daniel divulged could be called ghost-painting. A paints for B. Shows are conducted and B becomes a celebrated artist. The rich, the famous, the naive and gullible and many not-so-gullible are happy to buy such art pieces. Handsome payments are made.

She understood the game. Would she be comfortable playing it? Daniel said he had no regrets about this practice and felt happy.

Daniel said the first participation should be in a group show, then solo. It made sense. Media has to be taken care off to ensure the event featured in the art columns. Or at least it makes it to the Page 3s. And as she made her name the pricing would also be increased gradually.

The Principal was going to become an artist, a painter - to be launched within eight months, just before the annual holidays. She smiled to herself a secret smile of contentment. She slowly relaxed, then sank into a deep sleep. She could see an ocean of blue green on the one end, a beautiful reddish sky with grey on the other end of the shore. It was the rasping voice of the news anchor that broke her reverie. She hadn't heard the bell ring when Rajesh returned.

"Hello dear, sorry I am late, had your dinner?" Rajesh asked as he sat next to her to watch the news.

"Yes, darling how was the evening?" she was half asleep. "Nothing unusual, except one of my golf buddies is a little sad. His wife has almost decided they should separate. Their fights have been going on for long. Let them take a decision, the earlier the better. If they cannot get along, either adjust, agree or disagree it is a matter of understanding between both of them. I met the wife last week, a very tough lady, very hard nut to crack," Rajesh elaborated.

"I too was of the same opinion, you understand me. I work all day. After a hectic day, I cannot accompany you everywhere, we must give space to each other, be respectful and compassionate, that is important. One has to understand the sentiment of the other person. Thank God, we are different," Seema said with conviction. Ultimately, we each must be what we want to be in life. Rajesh took both her hands, held them in his palms, leaned forward and kissed her on her cheek. She could smell the alcohol in his breath.

"Looks like you have taken my share of the drinks. Please never cross the limit," she reminded him.

"Thank you, dear." She felt happy. He held her to wake her up.

They entered their bed room arm in arm. She was about to blurt out about her meeting with Daniel and the plan. She had always shared everything with him. But today she held back. 'No not now. It is still all in the air', she told herself.

Containing her excitement was difficult. So to stop herself from spilling the beans she quickly got into bed and tried to sleep. She knew she could do it even though time was limited. Why did she wait for so long? She chastised herself. Forget the past, what happened can't be undone, it is not important today.

Seema knew well the resources at her command. The school had nearly 1800 students, which made it a big potential. At least 500 students and parents would come for her shows. Of these at least 200 businessmen can be expected as visitors, many of whom could be art lovers. She needs do some homework and go through the parents' data which is in the computer. Or maybe she can ask her PA to compile the list of elite parents. 'Shall I announce my program in the kitty party? Oh no, that would be foolish and too early.' She murmured to herself.

"Seema, why aren't you sleeping? Is everything ok? Forget about kitty parties. Please sleep," Rajesh mumbled with so much love. Certainly, she would get a general opinion, feedback from the parents and visitors and so she will attend the exhibitions personally. Her head is saying 'Enough!' but she is unable to relax.

Chapter 2

Why was Daniel so frank? He said so many things without reservation as if he was waiting for an opportunity to open up and bare his heart. Who would not love him at first sight? He was talking like an innocent child, as if chatting with his mother. One day, this will be beneficial for both. She almost giggled with joy like a little girl.

Still, she had many doubts and no final answers. She could only hope for the best. As an orphan, he needs love. One thing he said was he lacks confidence. In school, some gossip about teachers always reached her ears but till date nothing against Daniel: that goes to his credit. Everything pointed to his goodness. He is married, yet he has not brought his wife to Delhi. Is it not a lame excuse that he doesn't have a house so he is not bringing her? That cannot be a reason. At least he has married. Both of her own children are yet not married. Whenever she talked about marriage, they had a ready answer, 'Mama please, wait till next promotion.' At their age, we were parents, which they don't realise.

One more thing to be ascertained: whatever he said had to be verified. She would keep silence for one or two days. She would certainly pay a visit to the art class, then recommend to the management for improvements, give more facilities to the art students and of course the teachers, and also initiate Daniel's housing loan. The last was just as important as the rest. Having mentally noted the jobs at hand she relaxed and peacefully slipped into a deep slumber. It had been an extraordinary day.

When the alarm went off at 5.30 am, she opened her eyes but still felt sleepy, wishing she could keep lying there for a little more time. She turned her body sideways, her eyes were staring at the wall. On it was a black-and-white photograph of her wearing her sari in her college days, sweet sixteen. It was the first time she wore the sari gifted by her grandmother. A wave of nostalgia hit her. Her eyelids were feeling heavy, she shut her eyes a little more. Her body demanded more sleep, a few more dreams. Then she remembered her ambitions. And admonished herself: 'Seema, you don't have time if you really want to be rich and famous. Before retirement, you have to plan the second phase of your life. An established artist. Right now there is no risk, no financial involvement, today you are in a position where the school can provide everything for you. Anyway, a great percentage of the credit for its popularity goes to you and your hard work'.

"Good morning, darling, you are late today. Are you okay?" Rajesh asked.

"Fine, darling. I did wake up but fell asleep again."

She raised her body and leaned towards her husband who was sitting by the bed doing his Pranayam. 'Brigadier Yogi' is what his friends call him for his passion for yoga and unaffected attitude – very content with his days in the Army, now just happy with his golf and scotch. It will have to be her to turn their retired life into a happening one. 'Today 'Madam Principal' tomorrow 'an acclaimed artist'.' The image in the mirror had a definite twinkle in the eyes. She was ready for the day.

Though she was a little late, the maid was ready as usual with her tiffin box. She knew Seema never shared lunch with anyone and stuck to a strict diet – sprouted pulses, two pieces of dates, four almonds and two vegetable sandwiches sliced into four pieces and seasonal fruit juice in a flask.

She finished her breakfast together with Rajesh. "Dear, I will leave a little late today for school."

"What happened? We did not sleep that late. Eyes are puffy. Any serious issue in school?"

"Oh no everything fine. I was just thinking about how to help our art teacher Daniel. He has been here since three years in my school, never realised he is so talented. Feeling guilty, management has not given him his due. We promoted only sports, theatre…partly I am also to be blamed. It all depends upon my own recommendations." Her voice echoing her remorse. "Never mind, dear, still time. You can always do something for him now."

She got up from the table, crossed over to his side and gave him the usual hug, and went for her bath. Brigadier was getting ready to go to play golf at the Gymkhana Club.

She was never late at school, her punctuality appreciated even by her enemies. Delhi International School was rated as one of the most sought after in Delhi. A proactive person, it was her initiative that made it the first school to recycle waste paper to art paper. In sports, DIS has been topping three years running and now would take up this new project in the most neglected department. Her sudden interest had to be justified.

Management will be willing and she did not want to raise suspicion among teachers, so she would let them also participate in the workshop. She decided that she would inform them after the morning assembly, when teachers meet for fifteen minutes. Her focus should be on art and providing for Daniel.

Her daily routine was to visit all the classes, meet the parents if any were waiting. Today the accounts officer would be called to project the financial requirements for art promotion. This is the only section handled by the Board Director Manish Malhotra's cousin Sukhdev Malhotra, a trusted middle-aged man. Till date he had never obstructed any decision she made. So she had nothing to worry about negative decisions once she makes the proposal.

Who else had to be kept under scrutiny? From the very beginning, she had decided to be careful because her closeness to one particular teacher would be carefully monitored.

The peon Naresh, her personal attendant, ensured she wasn't disturbed. A smart faithful and obedient man. He knew each visitor's importance and had been trained on how to deal accordingly: who was to be allowed and who was not. Once inside her cabin, Seema got busy with official papers to be dispersed and then shut her eyes. A lot of things were to be decided, a proper sequence of meetings would have to be established. In her meeting with Malhotra, there would be two more applications for housing loan -- one from an accounts department staffer, the other one a lady cleaner; the third to be included would be Daniel.

It was the right time, since his application could be processed along with the two applicants who were already in the list. This way no one can doubt her personal reasons for helping him. Even otherwise, he was a very deserving candidate. But why all of a sudden? That can raise eyebrows in the accounts department.

This is negative thinking, Seema scolded herself. She had been meditating for fifteen minutes, as she always did when any serious decision was to be handled. She would keep silent, shut her eyes, and do Pranayama for five minutes. Drink a glass of plain water and freshen up.

The colour of the light outside the door changed from red into green, for visitors a welcome sign. Peon Naresh heard the buzzer and walked in.

"Yes Ma'am, you need coffee or tea or shall I take the juice from flask?" "Give me a green tea only, Tulsi."

"And please call the art teacher Mr. Daniel. Call him first and make two teas. No wait, let him come, then make the tea."

"Ok, Ma'am."

Naresh bowed his head. He went to inform the art teacher in his class.

By the time Naresh arrived, Daniel realized it was not the usual call to meet the Principal; many times if there was any problem with students, then parents are called and teachers are also invited to the Principal's chamber. He was sure this time it is not for that and the reason had be about the last meeting.

"Daniel Sir, Principal Ma'am wants to see you at once."

After giving some sketching exercise to students and telling to the head girl to keep the class in order, Daniel left for the Principal's room.

He walked fast to reach her without losing any time. Naresh was waiting to open the door.

Daniel asked, "May I come in, Ma'am."

"Of course. Good morning, Daniel, how are you? Hope everything is fine."

"Yes, Ma'am, good morning,"

Chapter 2

"Yesterday we discussed many things. I was wondering how to proceed. But before I forget, the main purpose of calling you, did you prepare and fill up the form for the accounts department to apply for housing loan?"

"No, Ma'am. Earlier, I was not sure if the management will entertain my request. Today I will get the form filled. I need 8 lakhs and it will take me six years to repay the loan. An installment of approximately 10,000 per month is affordable and can be deducted from my salary.

"If the art market picks up, I may be able to repay faster. Actually the art market has already picked up; there is very big demand for masters. Hussain, Raza, Hebber and Jamini Roy – all are selling. The list goes on. Not to mention Raja Ravi Verma, Manjeet Bawa, Jatin Das, Paresh Maitey and Rameshwar Broota.

Among contemporary artists are Sanjay Bhattacharya, Jitesh Kallat, Riyas Komu, and Bikas Bhattacharya. The list is endless if you include upcoming artists. If you have any of their work, there are many buyers," Daniel gushed rattling off names of as many celeb artists he could recall.

"Nice to hear you are giving me such dreamy ideas to enter into a new avenue," Seema reciprocated.

"Please, Ma'am, you have to listen to me. This is the right time. Once you are out of the institution, you will no longer be in demand; when you are holding a position, then the recognition will be different." Daniel expressed his view with utmost sincerity.

"Exactly! That is exactly what I am thinking. We have to start implementing the idea from Day One," she concluded.

"OK Ma'am in your inner thoughts and in your sub-conscious or daily life what is the theme which you would like to paint? I mean realistic, semi-realistic or contemporary? Forget religious figures, flowers, landscapes, or portraits. Just give an idea, I will sketch that theme to which you can also contribute as per availability of time." Daniel was honest and very frank in his opinion. "Really, I am confused. If you ask for a theme, I love children. I mean, to start sketches," Seema said.

"Ma'am, you have to see the trend and people's perspective. To give an example: There was a time when Ganeshas did very well. Then came Radha & Krishna. Today Buddha is doing very well. Krishna is also picking up again."

The look of confusion on Madam Principal's face made Daniel stop and rephrase.

"Say fabric swatches. Are you aware designers plan the colours a year ahead? In case of art, it is no different. That is why present works have a time limit. Hussain, Tyeb Mehta Souza, Hebber and Raza all are great masters and the market they captured is steady even now, though hardly had any one of them is alive. If a man or woman artist had long struggle, very few among them succeed. They all made their market position.

Sculpture I am not discussing because it is not in our scope," Daniel said.

"All right, Daniel, give me a day. Today I have a management meeting after 3 pm. And give the application for loan pre-dated – at least a week back. Now I have to go through my old sketches. It's been many years, I have no idea where it all lie."

It was a white lie, one which Daniel was accustomed to.

"No problem. In the meantime, just send me an SMS or call, I will work on that theme.

Why I am interested in knowing the theme is because the other artists are all working on theme basis. There are others who take our help, their ideas should not clash with your ideas, we have to work on some unique theme," Daniel said earnestly.

"You are very right, Daniel," Seema replied, very pleased.

Naresh walked in with slip of a parent "Mr. Kapoor is waiting outside to meet Madam," he informed.

"Please send him in," she said.

Daniel stood up and left the room immediately. He knew he would get the housing loan as the Principal herself was taking the initiative. He felt blessed and it was a happy walk back to his class. The idea of Seemaji becoming an artist and he himself a house owner would be quite an achievement. Now the ball was in her court.

The noise from inside told him how the students were enjoying his absence. He was more than satisfied, in fact jubilant.

"Silence please!"

Usually, he got angry, did not tolerate indiscipline. But today was different. He was OK to let students have fun. He sat down for a while and requested them to show their sketches one by one. On second thoughts, he said:

"Listen, not to worry, please be seated, I am coming to every table. Keep silence please." His voice projected normal amount of anger given their unruly behavior.

He wanted to sit in silence just to mull over, and review all that he said to Ma'am, see if he made any mistake. She may enquire the name of the clients for whom he was working in the studio. If she wanted to see their contemporary themes he could not refuse. The only worry is his friend Surya is doing most of their work and his own involvement was rather limited. He had been waiting for the right opportunity and right person as his own personal client. Both the things happened together. A devout Catholic, Daniel knew it is all God's blessings. He silently sent up a thank you. He also wanted to thank Surya, his senior, to whom he was rather indebted. He had reached Delhi three years before him and was today an established artist.

When Daniel was frantically trying for a regular secure job, Surya stood by him and helped him as a good friend.

Today was very special: he felt infused with an unknown strength and confidence. A boy born out of wedlock. No one to call his own, except now Sarah, his young wife who was in Bangalore, waiting to come once he moved out of his shared bachelor pad.

He was bereft of parental love. Why was he in an orphanage? Till five years of age he has no memory except the nuns of Mothers of Charity and their blue and white sarees. His mother had found a safe place, a Catholic mission orphanage. As a young boy he was transferred into the care of Gabriel Brothers. He did not develop any attachment to anyone because they were always being transferred. Except Brother Vincent he had no consistent guide or mentor as Brothers were not allowed to single out anyone child.

He was convinced of one thing: his mother was a Keralite Christian and her name Mary. This information was provided to him after a great persuasion from a senior sister who currently lives in an old age home cum Retreat centre after her retirement in Lucknow. His mother's surname, was not mentioned and however, what perplexes him is how he become Ashok M Daniel when no one claimed fatherhood. Who is Ashok? Is Ashok his father? Does M means Mary? Is Mary his mother's name?

In college he had heard that many boys were named after their grandfather. Was Ashok his father's father? Or was he his mother's father? If they had so much sentiment, could he not have been brought up in his mother's house? Maybe his mother was married now, possibly she was not married when she conceived him. Someone might have questioned her virginity. So he was born to someone who must have been abandoned or deceived by someone. One thing is sure: he was an unwanted child at that point of time. Why did she not abort him? What prompted his mother and made her hesitate to do so? Maybe until the last moment, she would have hoped he would accept her. Or maybe he was married man, or his family might not have accepted her.

Never had he dwelt so much on his birth. He conjured up an image of a woman with a child much like the Virgin Mary with Jesus in her arm.

He sent her an unspoken massage' Never mind, Mamma, thank you for taking all the trouble to give me birth and keep me alive. You are a saint. You loved someone no matter what happened later. You are great, you fought a social war. Pregnant for nine months, unmarried, what humiliation you must have gone through.'

And he vowed to himself that one day he would find out the truth about his birth, the hospital, the place, the church, his Baptism, everything. But why all these thoughts today? Maybe because he was simply happy.

'When I got married, my wife did not bother to find out my genetic history. My priest, the Brothers under whose guidance and care I grew up, helped me and solemnised the wedding ceremony. Life time me and Sarah indebted to Br. Vincent and his cousin sister -Sr. Rosa the Mother Superior, who took the initiative for our alliance. Sr. Rosa was in-charge of St. Antony's Orphanage where Sarah was sheltered. None elaborated on anything about my parentage at that point of time. Today I am soul-searching to thank my mother, who gave me birth and because of whom I am alive today. She may be listening to what I am thinking, accepting the gratitude I feel in solitude.'

Till he reached home, he remained in a state of euphoria, even forgetting to lock his working table drawer. He was not even hungry. He just wanted to lie down, shut his eyes, and savour the moment all that happened today- is it all a dream? However, even though this haze of gratification had enveloped him, one question refused to fade away.

Is he taking a shortcut to achieve his goals in life? Oh no, he only said he can make her a popular artist and in return get his dues as a commercial artist. Is there any reason to be ashamed about? Is he killing his conscience? He knows his job, giving his work to a customer and getting paid. On the day of his graduation he had taken an oath - never fake anybody's work or forge a signature. Was he breaking his promise? Someone using his work: Is he at fault anywhere? The haze of happiness started to lift as doubts gnawed in.

He needed to reach Surya and discuss the outcome of the meeting. But won't that be a little premature? He got up and sat at the edge of his bed. He needed to be calm himself. Rein in your horses and wait. Only reveal to Surya that the home loan application has been submitted. Now he would not have any difficulty in paying at the time of allotment. He is now 28 years old, married a year back. Before 30, they will have their roof. Sarah will be thrilled, she has been counting the days when she would be able to join him.

Sarah too had been in the care of the Sisters for she too was an orphan, an abandoned child. Her education was in Madiwala, a small village near St. John's Medical College, in Bangalore. The Sisters at St Antony's got her from Delhi's Mother Theresa Ashram after V Standard, when she was shifted to Bangalore. Both their stories were more or less the same. Daniel was never interested to know much about her past except what she told him: she was just seven days old when found. Her mother lives in –Texas, work as a general nurse. Sarah knew that her mother did not want to be identified. There were no regrets from her side and she never felt the urge to meet her parents. It is not important today: a wedded couple are two individuals, healthy, good-looking, having enough to live on.

The only difference from other couples is that they did not get parental love or care. They lost the love of parents and childhood that any normal child has. During parent-teacher meetings (PTA), when parents came to the school to discuss academic performance and personal problems with class teachers, for them no one was there. Many times, he felt their absence, but Brother Vincent was there for him always. In class, Daniel used to spoil notebooks, last page and back covers of his classmates. Once his class teacher complained to Brother,

"He makes fun of everybody by making caricatures, cartoons, sketches". Brother Vincent replied,

"Okay Ma'am, if there are no serious complaints from fellow students, if they are happy, then don't bother".

"Oh no, I have great appreciation for his talent. He draws in all empty pages, sometimes he uses my drawing board and draws caricatures of his teachers before they enter the class. He is a talented boy, one day he will be an artist."

His class teacher was very honest in her statement. A smile hovered on his lips as he remembered his school days.

He shrugged off his old memories, squared his shoulders and stood up. Today, was like no other day. A great turning point in his life had come. Mentally he felt very calm and composed. He would have to climb the ladder of success like a child- step by step. He could not afford to fall or falter. There was no mother to encourage him or to lift him when he fell, no grandparents to hold his hand, to make him to walk. He had set his goal. He had to do something better than all his contemporaries. He was to be a celebrated artist.

Chapter 3

Today, Ashok Daniel had a fair idea of how he would have to proceed and make Madam Seema's journey as an artist successful. Reason: beyond doubt, when she became famous, a fair share of her success would certainly work in his favour. When he reached his office on Monday, he never dreamed the housing loan would be sanctioned so fast.

The accounts department entertained him well not as an ordinary staff.

"Mr. Daniel, you have to sign certain documents before August 15th. The amount will be remitted to your account, with an instalment fixed at Rs. 8,000 and a 8 years return period. Is it okay?" Surjit Malhotra asked.

"Perfect, thank you. Will you directly remit the money to the builder or will it be routed through my account?" Daniel asked, having no experience and never having availed of any loan from the school or any other agency.

"Not to worry, we are not bothered about the builder. You are the person taking the loan. We just need a certificate from the builder stating that you are the allottee of the flat. The total loan is Rs. 8 lakh. This is to make sure you are using the loan for its intended purpose. Moreover, management is fully convinced since Ma'am has guaranteed repayment.

"She strongly argued your case as a deserving one, and your credibility is well established by your performance over the last three years," Malhotra explained.

"Thank you for all the details; I'm very thankful," Daniel replied. He took the papers and studied all the conditions; nothing bothered him except one well-specified condition.

"You can't leave the organisation until you make the final payment." Malhotra reminded him. Was he signing a bond? On second thoughts, he realised it was very good; his service was assured for another eight years. It means that until the age of 34, everything is insured, like an insurance policy, with someone giving him a loan and making his life secure. Daniel was totally at peace. He would have to give everything he had. 'Ma'am is going to be a painter,' he murmured. She is a 'Painter-Principal', Daniel's mind reaffirmed.

The theme of Seema's first solo show is not important, he felt; she is a beginner. She has been a painter since her college days. With her husband's various postings in the Army, she was not able to devote herself full-time and establish herself as an artist. This would be a very convincing argument for the media, friends, and art fraternity as a whole. Her lifespan in the art field can be divided into five segments: 21–28 years; 29–35 years; 36–42 years; 44–49 years; and 50–55 years.

Like writers, creative artists have different moods, likes, and dislikes. They express their talent, and she too had her inner emotions accordingly. In the first phase, she painted flowers; in the second, she did figurative works; and in the third phase, she turned to nature, painting trees and birds. When she was in her mid-forties, human studies and portraits interested her, and now she's looking at contemporary landscapes.

For the present, she can paint Radha and Krishna for her solo show. People can judge from the period of her life whether she was joyful and effective. Her love, passion, inquisitiveness, talents, and experiments will be grist for the critic's mills. None will interfere, and Surya can decide what the critic will write. Daniel made up his mind on the specific themes. He wanted to give a surprise to the artist Seema of Delhi International School.

Surya can take up contemporary landscapes, and Daniel will do the Radha-Krishna Series for the group show. They have to formalise and finalise the shortlisted groups. Flowers, birds, landscapes, human portraits, and realistic works for that, they would have to add three more artists to their group. Then it will be an easy task, and we will have no issues. It should be a successful event.

Could he justify it? How do you group five themes or five artists? Many faces and many versions can create confusion and difficulties. He needs to discuss everything with Surya, who may not be in favour of involving many fellow artists in the first phase.

That evening, Daniel and Surya finalised their plan of action. They decided to have only 36 paintings on their list. It was a nice mix of flowers and nature, watercolours and charcoal sketches, human figures and portraits, realistic landscapes, and abstract and contemporary landscapes. Some work on Radha-Krishna combinations, one or two Buddhas, and a Ganesha for variety. Surya recommended the idea of Ganesha, 3' x 2' on acrylic, which would have an additional impact on the show. Surya thought a few religious themes in the beginning wall paintings, as well as her biographical data blown up in bromide prints, would work for the project.

Daniel, however, was not totally satisfied. He wanted something more to enhance the impact a little more.

"How about some write-ups from old art critics like Krishna Chaitanya and R.K. Yadav? Since they are no more, and one from Kesav Mallik, in which he can write about her current works." Surya was not so sure to begin with.

"We must try to do all this to make the effort more authentic. This is all we can manage, and one good reason for this is that none of the above critics are alive. We can easily manage hundreds of catalogue covers and comments from eminent and respected art critics. Let's just do a little search of old cartons." Daniel suggested it, as they had stacks of catalogues of exhibitions they attended.

By evening, the two had decided that they would not involve other artists. Surya will do contemporary abstract landscapes and a few sketches, and Daniel will do paintings of Radha-Krishna, Buddha, and Ganesha.

The duo decided that to make the exhibition more authentic, they would feature landscapes of hill stations like Lansdowne and Pathankot, where Seema and the Brigadier spent their early postings. But to prove beyond doubt the authenticity, some old sketch books showing scribbling ought to be there. Plus, some incomplete sketches for the media to document would help showcase her enthusiasm as a young painter.

Surya was a man of few words, very systematic, and reserved.

"Never do anything half-heartedly. If you do anything for anyone, do it with your heart and soul." That is the only reason that in the last ten years, even without any exhibitions to his name, he has been successful doing commercial assignments. Working for others provides no challenge and leads to a very peaceful, content, and settled life.

The period 2001–2013 was a glorious time for art and the art market. Even then, young artists were finding the going very tough, but Surya had no dearth of job offers. In the beginning, cash flow was poor. When he started doing commissioned work, he used to get only canvas, colour, and a small payment as an advance to begin the work. He used to take 3–4 days to finish one job and get Rs. 4,000–5,000 on average per job.

Daniel also helped out with the paintings. They never argued over the quantum of payments. They were more like brothers than college friends. Once Daniel landed the job and had a permanent income, the rent and rations were takern care of by him. His childhood in the orphanage had taught him that sharing was an important mantra of life.

"Anything you have in this world is not only for you, it is to be shared with the needy and, above all, with those who are near and dear." He recalled the simple letter he wrote to Surya, which now, in hindsight, looks a little silly. "Dear Surya, I would love to come to Delhi for a job. As the hostel rules say, I cannot continue here since my course is completed."

Surya's reply was a prompt, open invitation. "Who stopped you? Please come; you can be my roommate." Daniel will never forget Surya's warm welcome. Surya was very particular about certain things. Once he told Daniel "Listen, we are human beings who make mistakes, gossip, and indulge in loose talk. My survival depends on living up to the expectations and trust of clients, no matter who they are or what they do. That is purely their personal business. So please promise you will not share information about our clients outside this studio."

If Daniel agreed, they could stay together in Sangam Vihar, one of the densely populated, congested, unorganised, and unplanned colonies that dot the national capital. It is a community of skilled and unskilled labourers who work in various parts of the city.

Daniel appreciated Surya's concern and decided to share the two-room apartment, one of which served as a bedroom and the other as a studio on a 100-square-metre property, with a covered veranda converted into a kitchen, an Indian toilet, and a bathroom on the terrace. The owner was a Keralite by the name of Prakash, who earlier worked as an X-ray technician in a nearby hospital. Every month, Surya credited their monthly rent to his account.

The distance from the main road to their flat was approximately three kilometres down a rather narrow lane full of potholes and garbage dumps. When they invited their friends to their studio, it was always difficult to give directions in the absence of any prominent landmarks. The best way to reach them was to wait at the bus stop and get escorted from there.

At the bus stand nobody gets borred, within minute many people come and go and you can see a mini India. Sangam Vihar had become a veritable melting pot of the various cultures of the country. No one gets stuck there for long : it is like a corridor which pass skilled and unskilled labourers, and workers to different parts of Delhi and NCR. A thickly populated, conjusted colony. There is always push and pull to get into the bus.

According to Daniel and Surya, it was an ideal location for a documentary. "Stand there with a short video camera; you can shoot a small telefilm," they said. The whole cross-section of India is here. There is no acrimony; everything is orderly, even though there are no police to be found around."

"Is it not funny? No molestation on the transport bus," Daniel commented.

"Please don't make such an irresponsible statement. A bus with a capacity of 55 carries 125 people; see them on the footboards and the back carriage ladder at peak office hours, hanging on for dear life. Who cares if there is molestation or misbehaviour? These are all part and parcel of life. The first person who enters and the last person who is at the entry point become guards to the bus, and a person has to be strong enough to tightly hold onto the door railing. And others are almost simply hanging in the air, just holding their handbag or lunch box," Surya stated solemnly.

Daniel had experienced all these things but was just a little curious to know from his friend whether he agreed and endorsed his viewpoint. It may seem absurd, but that is the reality. It is hard to believe, but this is the plain truth," Surya stated.

"Why are people not condemning this situation and saying it is uncivilised and inhuman? It means everybody is enjoying the touch of the opposite sex, irrespective of caste and creed. Very secular, I must say!" Daniel retorted sarcastically.

"Oh no, dear, don't be silly! Until someone marries, it is all fine. But once they are married, they make faces about these things. To recognise a newly married man is easy: from his comments. They usually say, 'What's all this *yaar*? Please behave! You don't have sisters or a mother at home?' It means he has just been married. Otherwise, no one makes adverse comments, and the molester moves fast. No one is going to stay on the bus. Everyone is on the move. Who has the time to react? The culprit is rushing to find a way to get to his destination. And the victim, too, is in a hurry and has no time to object. It is a routine of to-and-fro exercise from 6 a.m. to 11 p.m., unending suffering. No one knows for certain if it was a genuine case of molestation or just a case of bodies rubbing against each" other because they are packed like sardines." Surya made his point. Daniel was learning fast from his friend's experiences.

Yes, that is it. You mean, it is just like public transport? Every passenger is harassed because 125 people are carted around in a 55-capacity bus!".

Even as Daniel's school schedule became more demanding, the friends' stimulating discussions continued. As is the case with most young people, the subjects for discussion were not about their immediate gains but bordered more on socialistic ideals: for the betterment of the country and, more importantly, how to save the country from the selfish politics of politicians. One morning, after listening to the current affairs programme on the radio, Daniel asked:

"Tell me, Surya, is our population not going to explode? Look at the population here in Sangam Vihar." His voice was filled with anguish.

"How can a nation progress at this rate? Every second, our population is increasing by one baby or more. How will we feed so many people?"

Surya's reaction was very calm. "Why are you being so serious? Remember what leaders say when they go on foreign tours? They have one slogan: 'Brothers, sisters, gentlemen, and ladies of the world, take the statistics. India has the youngest population. We can serve the whole world with manpower - skilled and unskilled. That is the slogan.

"Correct. Please stop your philosophising; we have to finish the work tonight, or it will not dry up by Friday."

Surya was in a hurry; Sunita Goyal's show was at the Taj Hotel on Saturday evening, and they were already into the middle of the week.

"Who will do the framing?" Daniel asked.

"Don't talk like a newbaby. The sizes are mostly in the 4' by 4' range. Framer has been told. By the time the paintings are done, the frames will be ready. Just fix it. The size is affordable for any average buyer. No artist can afford to keep their entire work in their studio or home. We have to be practical. Don't get confused; you read newspapers and listen to the news; it is all good as long as your stomach is full, you have a roof over your head, and you have clothes to cover your body. All this talk about what is good for the nation is good, so long as you have something to do with *rajneeti* (politics). Correct?" Surya was as logical as always. Daniel nodded in affirmation.

"Then why should you worry? First, it's *roti, kapda, aur makaan (food, clothing, and shelter)*. Did you understand the slogan? We crossed the bridge. Bread you have. Clothes are OK. Two pairs of jeans and three shirts are enough. Satisfied? Now about the house—you will also manage to get a loan. As for me, I never bothered much, you know? There is nothing permanent in the world. When have I had surplus money? I'm satisfied and happy, and there are no more requirements," Surya concluded.

"Please, Surya, you are always right, but sometimes give me a chance to make my point." Have you ever thought of getting married and starting a family?" Daniel asked.

"Family, yes, of course. I have a father, a mother, two younger sisters, and one younger brother, who is four years old. My father was very young when I was born. He was just 18 years old, while Ma was only 16. They still have time to make more babies!" Surya revealed his face, distorted with mock anger.

"Oh Jesus, don't talk rubbish; they are your parents, and still you are ridiculing them," Daniel argued.

"Not at all. You tell me, who will tell whom to stop? The leaders speaks of "young India, with 45% of the world's youth in India. 'Make in India' am I right? My parents are helping India become a progressive nation!" Surya's voice was dripping with caustic sarcasm.

"Listen, we can change the country; no media is with us, but we have art in hand. Make sensible, educational posters with messages and good slogans to control the population." Daniel made a responsible statement.

"It is easy for you to say that, as you don't have parents. I appreciate that you are an orphan; everybody cannot be like your father or mother!"

Daniel's face went ashen. He stood in stunned silence. Silence descended on the room. Surya realised what he had just said was insulting and humiliating. He was at fault. It was totally uncalled for. Nobody provoked anyone. Daniel was only asking out of concern. Surya should not have uttered the word orphan.

"Shame on me!" He jumped up, caught Daniel's hands, and held them to his chest. They were used to discussing everything under the sun, but hardly anyone spoke the truth.

"Please, my dear, I've crossed my limit. Please forgive me." Surya had tears in his eyes. Daniel's body was ice cold.

"In the future, we will never discuss any social or political issues except our work. It was a slip of the tongue; I should not have made this comment. I know everything about you, and still, I said something unpardonable."

Surya became very emotional but Daniel was the most understanding.

"My friend, here you have gone wrong; you spoke the truth. I felt bad, yes, but it is okay; never ever hesitate to tell the truth. Only then can we remain true to each other and build the value of a good friend."

"Agreed, but unwanted discussions bring enmity between friends. Relationships can break, so everyone must understand when and where one has to reveal the truth and where to draw the line."

"You are the only friend and relative I have after my beloved wife Sarah. Just forget it all. Today, no cooking; we will eat outside, my treat," its Daniel said and they reconciled. Both hurriedly got dressed and headed for their favourite restaurant near Batra Hospital run by a Keralite.

Chapter 4

Sitting at the small table in the far corner of the open-air restaurant, Daniel looked around and smiled to himself. It was a small *dhaba*-style restaurant, and as is always the case, even today it was teeming with activity. There was a large group of young ladies in their twenties and thirties, nurses working in the neighbouring hospital, chattering away in Malayalam, clearly their mother tongue. Other tables were dotted with young men and young couples. A crowd of men, mostly workers and labourers, were waiting their turn to get a seat for their evening meal.

Ramakrishna's Kerala Food was started in the early 1980s by an enterprising Malayalee couple who decided to tap into the need for cheap South Indian food that could cater to the burgeoning populace of nurses from the southern state who were joining the newly opened neighbourhood hospital. Today, the restaurant is popular not only among the denizens of South India but also among people from all over India and international students on the lookout for clean food on a budget.

Like every metropolis, Delhi is a bustling, sprawling city throbbing with life. Being the capital, all foreign embassies, all government undertakings, corporations, major banks, and United Nations Organizations have their offices here. In fact, most governments and international organisations have their head offices here. It is for this reason that the capital has turned into a cauldron of various cultures. Job seekers from all over the country throng here in search of better opportunities.

In recent years, the city has been witness to the mushrooming of multi-speciality hospitals. Health tourism has seen a big surge, with hundreds of patients coming from neighbouring countries, especially the Gulf and African nations. More hospitals have meant more opportunities for nurses and paramedics. Nurses from Kerala, acclaimed nationally and internationally, have thronged to the capital for better prospects.

The two artists soaked in the ambience and ordered their *thalis* of piping hot rice and sambar with little bowls of vegetables on the side. The warmth of the eatery owners and their relatives, who helped them run the place, pervaded the atmosphere as they went around serving and cleaning up after their guests with an air of happiness and camaraderie. Looking around, Daniels said, "Isn't this place a true picture of unity in diversity?" Surya acknowledged with a smile. The duo finished their meal and left their table in congenial silence.

"Tell me, Daniel, if the British had not united India for their political, administrative, or other purposes, the so-called colonial rule, would we ever have been united? We all might have been subjects of so many kings and queens of small kingdoms." Surya asked. Daniel's unity in diversity statement back at Ramakrishna's had him thinking.

"Sorry, dear friend, we had decided on a rule. No politics, no religious discussions with anyone at school or in public places," Daniel cautioned.

"Listen, I am not discussing politics, but like in your case, if your mother had not come to Lucknow, then the story would have been different. Please don't take it personally," Surya said.

"Absolutely, you mean if my mother would not have come, then where I would have been born. If there was not one united India, my father would have been a person from any of the three provinces of the Kerala under the Royals." Daniel said with a sad note and continued.

"Please, let's leave that topic. I was planning to discuss our principal's project. Anyway, a lot of things have been discussed. None of that is relevant; now there will be no more discussion except for our bread-winning project. Tomorrow's future is one of happiness and prosperity. Let us strive for it," he added. Surya, remembering the discord earlier in the evening, decided against pushing his views anymore.

"We have to finish twenty-four works of various sizes." As we discussed, Madam Seema has four themes that represent different eras of her life and moods," Daniel said.

"But before we start, let us have a meeting with Seemaji. If she likes the themes, either we go to her home or she can come to our studio," Surya interjected.

"Her coming here to our studio? Isn't that impractical? For a principal to come to our studio, park the car in front of the Batra Hospital and get an auto or cycle rickshaw to reach here. Her driver would have plenty of stories to gossip about. Especially drivers, they have four eyes and four ears!" Daniel declared with a grimace, "It will be very embarrassing. She hardly has time to spare for this project. It was I who prompted her to hold her show. She's not like Sunita Goyal; she's not that bold. When I proposed the idea, she was silent."

"You mean her coming to our studio is ruled out; it would expose her?" Surya said.

"Exactly like we are doing for others, she will, of course, bear the cost of whatever is needed." It was a harmless lie. Daniel had never discussed anything with Seema about finances. He was ready to invest the amount in the hope that she would reward them. At least he is getting a loan for the flat; when you get a loan from anywhere, there is a certain processing charge and of course time saving.

As usual, both took tea before the night's sitting commenced. "You know, Daniel, this kettle has great sentiments to it. I bought it with my first earnings for 150 bucks," Surya said. There was a look of great satisfaction on his face while he mentioned the kettle.

"Okay, then, you work on two themes of her younger days, and I do the two series of her 14-year-old period; two subjects: abstract series and semi-realistic series," Surya assured of his valuable contribution.

"The sketches are important before proceeding further to the painting stage. The whole idea is to project her versatility and her active life as a professional. How her husband's transfers stood in her way of holding regular shows. It has to be convincing, and we have to select the canvas and sketch papers. As for being authentic, finding out about the old sketches is not that difficult. Even the old discarded canvas can be used for paintings," Daniel added.

"Look, the sketch is old; the canvas is old, but what is the medium—water colour, charcoal, acrylic, or oil?" Surya asked, now totally focused on the job at hand.

"I don't think that will be a serious issue," Daniel was so assertive, but Surya was not convinced.

"Look, the public are not fools; invitees and artists can make sarcastic comments. You know what happened at the National Art Fair: a reputed gallery displayed Jamini Roy's works on a 2' x 2' canvas on acrylic. A visitor made a valuable comment, and the representative came and stopped him from taking photographs. In Jamini Roy's time, there was no acrylic colour, and above all, the canvas looked so fresh. This is what I heard. Think it over. Visitors at art exhibitions are serious visitors, and most of them know what art is," Surya persisted.

"I appreciate your views, so we will make it very simple. For her earlier works, you only take drawings and sketches in charcoal or crayons, then spray them for preservation.

"I will do the last 7–8 years of her work. In the last three years, I have known her, you know that. So there is no difference in opinion: we should be careful, as usual. No friends or visitors come to the studio till the assignment is over," Daniel said.

"But Mukesh is coming over now," Surya agreed.

With the discussion over, both remained in their respective workspaces, quietly contemplating and waiting for Mukesh. While Surya, like always, drank his hot tea, Daniel sipped at his cup as though he were eating the tea, as a slow eater would.

"Why is Mukesh taking so long?" Daniel asked, looking at his watch.

Surya's friends and fellow artists, like Mukesh Kumar, would drop by often. Many a time, they would sit and chat into the wee hours. And Daniel always looked forward to these chat sessions because this was when he gained great insights into the current art market, artists, art lovers, and auction houses. He was still a newcomer in the trade, and he was quite impressed by Surya's knowledge of the art world and all the behind-the-scenes goings-on.

"How many celebrity artists' homes have you been to?" Daniel asked. Though it would seem like an idle query, he was hoping this would get Surya to reveal information about the artists and their world. He knew Surya had accompanied framers, posing as their assistant.

"I don't want to name them, but from the work that's lying around, you can easily figure out who all I have been able to replicate," Surya replied with an impish smile.

Celebrity artists usually do not allow outsiders to enter the studio, except framers, who supply the stretchers, canvas, and relevant materials. The framers often ask their trusted artists to accompany them to the homes of celebrities on the pretext of being assistants at his workshop. The framers take advantage of the opportunity to prolong the time at the studio so that the person accompanying them can study the colours, styles, variations, and all other details that can be used when copying the work. While the framer engages the celebrity in a conversation, asking many questions and seeking clarifications, the copy artist studies the celebrity's palette, colour, brush size, and techniques.

"You know, framers are very particular about selecting copy artists. They only take those they can implicitly trust and who are not too greedy. And framers like Ram Prakashji are quite knowledgeable. They can figure out the quality of the canvas used, the brand of the brushes, or the colours. Unless it is very badly required, the framer doesn't take the copy artist to the senior artist's home". he added.

Mukesh, who had just walked in, pulled up a stool and joined the discussion.

"The general impression is that the framer is the culprit, and he is responsible for the fakes in the market. But actually, there's a long conspiratorial network involved behind the curtain. It took almost three years for me to come to a conclusion: it is a chain of conduits, a network—from the senior artists to the framer to the gallery owners and the auction house."

Surya explained that senior celebrities want to be in the limelight. They attend parties and events to ensure they get featured in the Page 3s and Saturday supplements of national dailies. Visiting gallery opening discussions and late-night parties hardly leaves time to work—after social calls, travel, and parties. How can they manage to spend time in the studio? Though it is hard to believe, there have been incidents where the framers kept the original and the artist got the duplicate. So exceptionally good were the copy artists that the celebrities were unable to recognise their own work. The truth is that it is very difficult to differentiate good copies from the original. When the copy masters are at work, they are very particular about knowing the year of the work so they can use the same style and technique; the colour code needs research.

"The buyers who buy these copies well know they are not buying the original because they are buying it for a song. They are not art lovers. They only love to hang paintings of celebrities, as it elevates their social status. These people would not spend one-tenth the money on buying an original work by an unknown artist. Unless the framer gets 100 percent confirmation from the buyer for a particular artist's work, he never takes a chance on reproduction.

The gallery owners, the framers, and the copy artists have great teamwork, and meticulous planning with high precision that goes into every reproduction. Once the photocopy of the duplicate works is done, it is matched with the senior artist's work and printed simultaneously. Every effort is made to match it centpercent perfect. The public is then given a combination of the original and copied prints so that there is no confusion in the market and no negative feedback emerges from either direction. As a practice, they take 50–100 prints of the work and sign them as 8/50 or 5/100 for people who cannot afford an original. These copies are available at many gallery outlets.

This is trial and test print so that there will not be any adverse comments from the market. After this, they will become very confident, the celebrity artists original work they copied and its prints then become genuine work.

Daniel sat there quietly, soaking in all the information, much like an empty canvas being splashed with colours. He did not want to butt in and pose any questions, though he was getting quite distressed by his seniors' nonchalant attitude. Why devote so many years to the study of art if, in the end, you want to end up being just a copy artist? Where is the moral fibre of these young artists? How come they don't revolt against this system that's cramping their natural style and expression and reducing them to mere duplicators? And how much do they make? Unable to stop himself any longer, he blurted,

"How? Oh, how does a senior artist not recognise whether the work in front of him is his own or a copy?"

Both Surya and Mukesh turned around to face Daniel as though he were the dumbest person on this planet.

"Daniel, have you ever taken cow milk from the village side?"

"Yes."

"Have you ever asked the milkman how many teeth his cow has?"

"No." "Then why are you so curious and anxious to know about what is happening in the art world?" Here the question remains: "Who is genuine?"

Daniel kept quiet. To find out more, he needed to be a patient listener so that there would be no discontinuation in the conversation. Like a child, he was so curious to hear stories. Surya was in a good mood. He had already opened his bottle of Scotch, gifted by his clients. He was speaking with a lot of authority, and Mukesh was not contradicting him, which made for an authentic account. Daniel felt he was in court, listening to a judgement being pronounced.

"Who is genuine?" Surya repeated, throwing his arms wide in a dramatic gesture.

Everyone wants to hear the story straight from the horse's mouth.

"Surya, you had two large ones; at least you say who is genuine and who is not." Mukesh asked.

After a moment of silence, Surya said, "The question is: are we genuine and honest?" "Yes, we are," he answers himself and continues.

"Yes, we do copy. For reproduction, we select the best canvas, good-quality paint, and a good brush. We do our best, and we are paid. That is the first phase: we are genuine and honest. Now the framer never fails to pay 50% in advance before he takes the work from me. Is he not genuine? If the gallery owner is not honest, how does Ram Prakashji pay us the advance payment?" He stopped and took a sip of his drink.

"How do you know the original work by the senior celebrity is genuine?"

Unable to fathom what Surya meant, Daniel burst in,

"It is the original work by the senior, so it has to be genuine!"

"We call them senior celebrities. But do you realise they all have assistants? There are many Katarias, Jayant Phules, and Aroras. Don't you know they are accommodated in a senior's house and are very well paid? First, you call this so-called artist a helping hand to assist seniors at their studio. They play a sincere role in doing the best for their master. Do you understand now what is happening?"

"You mean to say all the celebrity artists over 70 are not actually working?" Mukesh always interrupts.

"Yes, my friend, a good percentage of them are sick : Alzheimer's, chronic diabetes; some are bedridden; others are full-time socialites. Their work sells like hot cakes, even before they are ready. Even before the paint dries, takers are there to carry it to galleries. It would take three generations to complete the number of such works floating around in the art world. Did you not visit the last art exhibition at Okhla?" Surya asked.

"Yes, we were all there," Mukesh replied.

"What have you seen and experienced? A great show, big publicity—am I right? I just narrated the Jamini Roy episode to Daniel. The gallery owner did not allow photography. Remember how the photographer laughed? 'Jamini Roy's work in acrylic? Hilarious! And the paint is yet to dry!' I saw the gallery owner's face go pale. All are honest; everyone was paid for their labour."

"So you mean to say that, except the buyer, everyone is genuine?" Daniel asked.

"Come on, Daniel, you are still a child, Buyers are the most genuine people, their conduits enquire, 'Original or copy?': Once they know the price, they say I don't need the original; it's just for my drawing room or dining hall, or my boss wants to give a gift to a bureaucrat in the Income Tax Department. He is a very honest person and never takes bribes. Poor man, his wife is always happy to receive a painting of celebrities like Hussain, Raza, or Hebber as a gift, to which the honest bureaucrat has no objection. Who loses? No one, everybody, is honest to the core!" Surya ended with a sigh.

The night was still young. Daniel got up and walked onto the open terrace while Surya and Mukesh sat puffing their cigarettes. He needed the fresh air to clear his head. Surya's barrage of information had sent him into a tailspin. He walked up to the other end of the terrace and leaned against the parapet wall. Is this to be his fate? Copy artist for a well-known senior? To die an unacknowledged, uncredited death? His talent is unsung. His upbringing by the brothers clearly did not equip him for this fake and phoney art world. He didn't know how long he stood there, lost in the loss of his beautiful, guileless world, when he heard his name called out. He looked up to see Mukesh beckoning him.

Chapter 4

"Why are you outside?" Turning to Surya, he said, "Please tell Daniel the time when our octogenarian, Ismail Sahib, left the inauguration of his exhibition."

Surya wore a mischievously wicked smile. He was pacing the floor in a theatrical fashion, building up the drama.

"This incident will tell you what can happen if the senior celebrity is not paid on time. Their fate will be like that of the Nai Dilli Gallery. The gallery was celebrating his 1980s-era collection of 20 paintings. Brochures, publicity, and media for interviews are to be followed by wine and cheese. The old man was a little late, as usual. His assistant, Jayant Phule, was pushing his wheelchair to the centre of the hall. Any moment, the great show of the celebrity would be inaugurated. It was an anxious yet electrifying moment. Art lovers, young and old, are waiting for a glimpse of a celebrity who rarely appears in public because of his age. Photographers were clicking cameras with their flashlights blinking." Surya paused. A dramatic pause. "But he came and went without attending the inauguration or meeting the media."

"But why?"

"Because the gallery had not made full payment for his work." Or should I say his assistant's work?

"I can't believe this!" "You can't be serious."

"Well, let me finish. Then you judge. Ismail Sahib reached the lobby. We all went and touched his feet and kissed his palm. He is not in a position to lift his arm and needed someone to help. Some were lifting his hand and themselves, putting it on their heads for blessings. It was a sight to be seen. Phule showed such patience. I was watching him. The look on his face was as though he too wanted everyone to touch his feet. I am sure he is thinking, 'Bloody, I do the work, and everyone wants to touch his feet. Do the people not have eyes to see that it has been 12 years since his stroke, he is wheelchair bound, and he cannot even raise his arm?' Have you not noticed his assistant enjoying all the drama, the socialite ladies, and how some women artists would casually rub him with their breasts and buttocks—carefully careless? No matter; every dog has its day. One day, the assistant will also have the same fun. Wait and see." Surya finished in one breath.

The wheelchair moved from wall to wall, with the photographers alongside. Ismail Sahib raised his left arm slightly, and Phule bent his head. In a whisper, he asked in his ear, "How many work—twenty, is that right?"

"Yes, sir, twenty confirmed," Phule said.

"Ask them to wait for the lighting of the lamp; take me to the washroom."

People who know him are aware of all his habits. Before any inauguration, he goes to the washroom because he has to spend a lot of time in the gallery with media, discussions, interviews, and cocktail parties, so he wants to be at ease for long hours.

"Where is Sudeep?" He enquired.

"Sir, I have also not seen him. Only his girlfriend is here."

"What has she promised you?" The senior asked.

"Balance will be paid at the time of inauguration. Now he is missing. I asked Miss Namrata. he said there was an urgent call to get home. His mother wasn't feeling well. So everything was left to her," he concluded.

With great difficulty, Ismail Sahib pulled Phule's head towards his mouth and murmured into his ear.

"Did I not warn you that before you deliver all the work, he must make full and final payment?" Senior was angry.

"Sorry, sir, he paid 30%; the balance, 70%, he said he would pay at the time of the inauguration when we reach here," Phule stammered.

"Don't worry, take me to the lift, call the driver, and we will go home."

Surya enacted the scene like a gifted monologue actor. "We all waited, but he didn't return. The show was finally inaugurated by a professor from the College of Art. And what did the media report? Because of a medical emergency, he was rushed to the hospital, and the show was called off. Who reported? Media. Are they all honest, paid pimps? Are we all honest? Honesty! Who found out the truth? Worthless, meaningless—am I right? No, no more discussion today." The group disbanded for the night. Daniel secretly hoped they'd have another session like this soon. As he listened to his friends revelations, he found he knew very little about what was going on in the art world.

Chapter 5

Sleepless nights have different meanings for different people. It varies from person to person. But for Daniel, though he slept late, still he was not tired. In fact, he felt more energetic, with no feeling of tiredness due to the late sleep and short hours in bed. The day was different from all these past four years of life: Madam Seemaji was waiting for him. He must be more disciplined look and he must shave which he did only once a week in the past. From today, he had to change his routine, a new beginning.

His excitement was palpable. Madam Seemaji may call him to discuss the charter of action that they left at last night's dinner table. What if she were to turn down his proposal? Why this negative feeling? He chided himself. "Think positive." She had agreed in principle to the housing loan that she recommended. With her recommendations, the management would never refuse. Seemaji is a towering personality among all the principals of Delhi schools. That is why she could earn a commanding position on Delhi International School's Board of Governors and earn the trust of trustee members.

She is so enthusiastic about establishing herself in the field of art. And she has to do it in a short period of time. The question is how much time she can devote by leaving aside her most responsible position. Can she ignore the school and daily routine? Daniel had offered whole-hearted support, service, and his talent, which she accepted with great happiness. He can only hope there is no change in thoughts. Let him not pre-judge, and time will bring the course of action. But he must be prepared for the call at any time; anxiety prevailed.

While he was in his classroom, he ensured that his expression did not betray the extra privilege he received from the principal. With all seriousness he instructed and guided the students, he was fully alert, expecting a knock on the door from the peon at any time. There was a knock, but much later than he had anticipated. He walked to the door slowly, making sure his eagerness was not obvious. The door opened, but instead of Naresh the peon, it was Mrs. Richa from the sculpture department. He was surprised. Never before did fellow teachers come to the classroom for any discussion during class hours unless there was something serious.

"Hi. Sir, yesterday you were busy; I saw you, accompanied by the peon, going to the principal's room. I hope everything is fine. Anything to do with our department, my art section?" A lengthy question, many doubts and enquiries compounded.

"Hi Richa! Nothing serious. Principal Ma'am wanted to start an orientation programme for all teachers to join for painting three days a week for two hours a day. I was thinking of discussing this with you after the lunch break. "It is not compulsory; everyone who wants to join is welcome; it is for anyone who is interested in art," Daniel explained.

"That is OK. It is nice to hear that at last Ma'am has recognised our department; otherwise, her focus is always on sports and games. The art market is booming; that can be a reason," Richa said.

"It is too early to comment. We will wait till she calls us for a discussion," Daniel said.

"Is it only for painting department or any mention for sculpture course? Shall I prepare anything?" Richa was very inquisitive.

"No idea, Richa; you know that in three years, this is the first time I was called, and you have only completed two years," Daniel said.

"No, I have completed two and a half years," Richa answered.

"Ok. Let us meet after the lunch break." Daniel did not want to reveal anything more to Richa.

The principal had not mentioned the sculpture department; if clarification is required, let Richa speak to her directly. He must remain with his department; it is not necessary to start a campaign, Daniel told himself.

Ashok Daniel was a little puzzled. So much had been discussed that, as is normal, there should be some feedback from her side. There was a big gap to be filled. To become a painter, her childhood testimonials were needed, and making some sketches and paintings was important.

She said during her school days, Seemaji used to help her classmate Sunita Goyal in art class. It was evident that this was an unfulfilled ambition. It all led to one goal: she had to establish herself as a painter, a known artist. How the hell can she spare time on her routine? When can she devote her time?

There is only one option: someone must help, associate with her, or tutor her for this long journey. Considering the eagerness she has shown with full awareness, a methodical approach must be worked out to fulfil her dreams.

Still, two hours remained for lunch. He had to be patient. He could not let doubts cloud his mind. He pushed all negative thoughts aside and decided to enthusiastically concentrate on his class and his students. Teaching art to this group of youngsters was a challenge. They were all teenagers. In art class, when doing anatomical sketches, their awkwardness about their own changing bodies became most evident. Daniel had to handle this class with care. He immersed himself in guiding his students.

Soon after the lunch break, he received the one-page typed note about the orientation for the art workshop, titled a 'Circular' for all staff concerned. The content was short and simple.

The principal and management had decided to have art workshops three days a week for two hours each day on Tuesday, Thursday, and Saturday between 2.30 and 4.30 pm. All interested staff may contact Mr. Ashok Daniel, Art Faculty Head.

Chapter 5

Oh, God! A little while ago, he was underestimating the calibre and efficiency of the Principal's wildest thought. She has moved so fast on turning the idea into reality.

The dilemma now is what to do with Richa, as there is no mention of the sculpture department. Maybe she is aware that the sculpture market is not doing well in India and might have deliberately avoided it. Richa should not feel he had any role in this new development. At the end of the typed note, there was a handwritten note: 'Meet me after class', signed Seema Chopra.

The letter is from the office, and the possibility of a meeting at the residence cannot be ruled out. Certainly, things are moving as anticipated. As for the art orientation course, it remains to be seen how many staff members are going to attend. Most of the school teachers have their own priorities, like private tuition, and some have side businesses like shops and automobile workshops. Women teachers tend to run home after class as household affairs are their responsibility.

He must at least enrol five to six teachers, then the workshop can be justified. The situation would not become awkward—the principal took the initiative, and what if no one responded? Some of the staff who are close to her will certainly join only to please Ma'am. They will be at her disposal by offering evening services for vegetable buying and groceries for the house, taking care of blouses and skirts, and knitting winter wear in advance. Sincerely, none of this middle-aged set is serious because he knows them; then, how will the class be effective?

This can always materialise, provided they get an incentive. Who will suggest it? It all depends on the interest in joining the class, and someone may join for remuneration—that is the only key issue; otherwise, art will remain only for the artists' sake. Unless the principal can recommend some ex-gratia payment apart from their salary, such an incentive might be needed for the plan to take off.

The workshop got underway and quickly became a hit. There were teachers from both junior, high and senior high schools. Daniel didn't want to consider the rationale of their participation. He was pleased to see Seemaji occasionally participate. She made use of the class to spread the word that she had always been interested in the arts.

On a parallel course, Daniel worked tirelessly on making Seema's debut in the capital's art world a success. His efforts fared well. She became a known figure in the capital's art circuit. Her three group shows and a one-woman show, which the media highlighted as a new entrant with a lot of promise, gave her ample publicity. She met many personalities, VIPs, and politicians and exchanged visiting cards, mobile numbers, and contacts. However, there was no time for socialising. The most intimate friends and relatives are invited to cocktail parties, where sometimes only wine and cheese are served.

Daniel, however, did not attend any of the openings. He and Seema had an unspoken but clear understanding that he should not be present during the opening of the show. Though deep down he felt hurt, he kept up appearances and never expressed regret or disappointment. There are always buyers and the media. He missed them all. So the opportunity to meet new clients and prospective buyers was rare.

The next day she would narrate in great detail all that happened at the opening and was eager to know if her exhibition was a success from his feedback of the media and TV coverage that he was asked to watch by her.

From the second day on, after school, he had to be in the gallery; that was mandatory. "Daniel, please see 8.30 pm today on Aajtak or NDTV'. It had become necessary to watch, record, and find out to know about every visitor who was present. Over the last two and a half years, he has collected paper cuttings for 8-9 shows, and media video tapes so that he can see, study the viewpoints and the opinions—can you recall the people who are regular visitors -- who's who from Ma'am's contacts and her well-wishers during the exhibition period.

"Daniel, I need you to be there. Sometimes serious visitors and buyers may visit. You can better explain and handle them," Seemaji used to tell him. As she became established, footfall saw a gradual increase. There were a few regular visitors, of whom two interacted with him the most. Both were ladies. They were very casual; they walked in and spent a good deal of time in the show, interacting and asking many relevant questions about the paintings. They were serious art lovers.

Many times, he noticed one thing in common: they avoided entering their name in the visitor's book and signing. As a curator, he could not ask for details about visitors unless they voluntarily disclosed them or came forward to introduce themselves and write in the visitor's book. Very soon he realised that one of them was Mrs. Meena, wife of a Cabinet Minister and the other was Sunita Goyal, one of Surya's client. Both the individuals' questions were common and genuine. Their appreciation had a common pattern. They ask, "Your name?"

"Daniel."

"Hope you are an artist, a freelancer, or working with some institutions."

"Yes, I am a teacher in the art department."

To avoid damaging Seemaji's reputation. He must ignore more questions and answers which can lead to unwanted information. Compared to Sunita, Meena Singh was very clever while asking questions. Once she asked,

"Where is your studio? I am a fan of your work. I am highly impressed with some of your earlier work seen on Facebook."

"I am grateful; thank you so much."

"Why are you not participating in the show?" Mrs. Singh asked again.

"Sorry, ma'am, this is a solo show by our Principal," Daniel replied.

Then and there, he realised he had spilled the beans. He had revealed that he was an art teacher at Seemaji's school, DIS, where she was the principal. Mrs. Singh gave a beautiful smile, looking at him intelligently without explaining, as if she knew he was working for Seema. From her observations, it was clear that the ladies were on a fact-finding mission. From past experience, they are regular visitors and spend no more time than a usual visitor. At that point in time, he never felt any doubts. Any question is a puzzle. Why did they avoid the inaugural day or opening day of the exhibition? Maybe they are not interested in the crowd which is enjoying a bash of wine and cheese. Both of them never asked for any details about the artist Seema's whereabouts or expressed any desire to meet the artist.

Sunita came and went fast—hardly fifteen minutes—as if coming there to assess the success of the show and the number of works sold. On the other hand, Meena Singh was meticulous; her questions were well prepared.

"How was the opening? The Hindustan Times covered the programme very well. The write-up and the review were very good," Meena appreciated.

"Thank you, Ma'am. I believe you too, are an artist because you spend good time seeing and appreciating the work." Daniel casually replied.

"It's not very serious; I was a school teacher and just took it as a hobby, but I love to visit shows. Of course, I paint, though not on a regular basis," Meena said.

"Ma'am, can I have your contact telephone number and email address so that we can invite you to the next exhibition?" Daniel did not want to lose the opportunity to get her full ID so that his doubts would be confirmed.

"I appreciate it but I don't want publicity as my husband is a cabinet minister," she replied. A very hard nut to crack, he noted. Daniel found she was feeling a little uneasy. If she is a politician's wife, then they are public figures. Visiting an art gallery is not a crime. Why the hell—she moves very consciously and always finds one or two men in civil dress walking in before her visit?

Chapter 5

They follow her at a distance; when she leaves the place, they too accompany her. Daniel moved out on the pretext of going to the bathroom. He waited outside.

There are fewer visitors on weekdays, her car was in the parking lot, and he didn't take long to figure out who was who from the body language of the gate watchman. He could figure out that she was a VIP. He got the name of the minister and the cabinet post from the watchman. He went to note down the vehicle number and details—when accompanied by bodyguards, free car parking is the privilege of cabinet ministers and bureaucrats.

When he walked in, he saw she was chatting with Sunita Goyal. He noticed that they happened to be there for their usual chats. As usual, Sunita wished him with a casual expression. There was no sincerity in her words or in her body language.

"Mr. Daniel, this show in the capital is a great success; it looks like seven works were sold on the first day. May I know who the buyers were so that I can also invite them to my next show at AIFACS (All India Fine Arts and Crafts Society)?" Sunita said.

"Sorry, Sunitaji, the first day of opening I was not here and Madam Seemaji has the buyers' names; if you leave your contact information, I will convey your message," Daniel answered very innocently.

"Not to worry, it is okay. If not with you, it is fine." Sunita commented.

As Sunita moved away, Meena called out to her and stated:

"By the way, Sunita, Mr. Daniel is working with Seema Chopra at her school."

Daniel had not given any serious thought to that statement. These two great ladies were trying to corner him and wanted to extract some details about him and Seemaji, about her studio, and about her working hours. As usual, Sunita took a round, spending more time with the works sold, marked with a red dot.

"Meena, I have to go for another opening of Kalicharan's show at Habitat."

"Yes, fine. I may spend a little more time here." Meena said. Soon after, Sunita Goyal left.

Meena was buying time to linger on; it was visible on her face.

There was a hidden agenda, and he could expect many more questions in the offing. He would have to be cautious when responding, using as few words as possible.

He walked towards his table. On the pretext of opening the visitor's book, Meena came and sat across the visitor's chair.

In a friendly manner, she asked: "If you don't mind, are you from Kerala? Which part?"

"No, Ma'am, I am from Lucknow, born and brought up there. After my graduation in BFA fine arts, I migrated to Delhi," Daniel replied.

"From your look and appearance, I was under that impression... but your language seems like a North Indian's."

"All your assumptions are right. My mother is a Malayalee, and I was brought up in a Christian boarding school with Keralite priests and brothers. Thank you, Ma'am. I never realised I looked like a Keralite."

"Your parents?"

"Mother, I have no idea, and father is a mystery. Till date, I have never met them." When the parentage issue comes up, he is always blunt. Never leave any ground for further questions, which is why he never tells a lie, let the truth prevail. He felt Meena Singh wanted to have a lengthy conversation. Willingly or unwillingly, he was also happy to spend time with her without visitors. Sitting in the gallery alone is boring. He had the time and inclination to carry the conversation further. She was a cabinet minister's wife and would certainly be influential. An acquaintance can be a future client; after all, an artist's survival is purely on the basis of contact. Later, they become promoters. There is nothing wrong with meeting new people, he told himself. She was silent for some time.

"Ma'am, can I offer a cup of tea or some water?"

"Don't bother. I see you always with visitors, some people around, so I thought not to disturb you. I avoided talking to you," Meena said.

"Not at all, you are always welcome."

"I'd like to see your works, love to see your studio and see some of your recent works. I am an amateur and have a long way to go."

"Thank you, ma'am; my studio is not in a good neighbourhood. It's in Sangam Vihar, the roads are not very approachable. But I am planning to shift very soon," Daniel replied. There was no option left to avoid her visit, which might bring uneasy experiences. If she sees the works of different styles and assignments of different forthcoming works, she may think we are cheap and can be bought.

"It is okay, Daniel; we are experienced with alleys and lower income dwelling places. Real voters never live in posh housing, always live in unauthorised and slum areas. Though I asked you, it may not be immediate." One of my staff members will visit your place and study the location. We cannot simply move into places without this so-called security and safety code. No matter, just give the address. When I visit, you will be contacted in advance," Meena said.

Already, she has his mobile telephone number; she wants the address, no way can he refuse. If she calls, he can lie about being "busy" or "out of town." Without any hesitation, he gave the address. One thing he could not help thinking: 'See who is asking for the telephone number. It is certainly a great day. This relationship, if it grows, will give ample opportunity for exposure to the media and open up a good social circle. But my ambition is not hinged on the expense of others; it is founded on merit and hard work.'

The only question that bothered him was why he was denied the opportunity to attend the inauguration or preview. Seemaji kept him busy with various tasks for one reason or another, making sure there was something going on at school or that there was an orientation session.

Nevertheless, despite missing out on the opening day, Daniel was always content Seemaji would call as soon as he reached home from the gallery.

"Hi. Daniel, dear, your hard work and help paid dividends. Please watch the 9.15 pm Art World channel. The Hindustan Times and Times of India also covered the programme. Before you go to sleep, call me. I need your feedback if I have said anything out of line in my interview," Seemaji said.

"Yes, Ma'am, I do," Daniel said.

"You are the only one I trust, and whoever trusts me, I never let them down, Daniel," she said affectionately.

"Yes, Ma'am. Good night".

"Had your dinner?"

"No, I was waiting for your call to know the outcome."

"Everything is fine. Have your dinner and see the programme. Call me, however late it may be."

"Yes, Ma'am."

Sarah is always a silent witness to all these conversations. Her displeasure about his not being invited to participate with Seemaji on opening day, as if he was an outcast was palpable but never voiced.

"Then who are you to report the outcome "she used to scold him.

Though she was an orphan girl, she was aware of the extra privilege and liberty authoritatively exercised on her husband by Seemaji. The gifts, saris, and semi-precious jewellery that Seema sent whenever she went shopping were always appreciated as a kind gesture. Sarah never made any adverse comments; she merely expressed her gratitude.

But today, for the first time in their five years of married life, she made her displeasure obvious.

"I've been calling you for dinner since 8 p.m.; you're just delaying it until 9 p.m. Why, dear, is it so important to wait and know about the opening of Madam's show? You worked day and night and did all the hard work, when not even for one inauguration have we been invited?

Then who are you to report the outcome? In all art fraternities, your friends are always invited. Why are we ignored?" '

"Sarah, look, you don't understand; it's a coincidence. She gives me some work—an assignment for school. You cannot call it being ignored or deprived; it is a part of life and the job," Daniel said.

"Please, Daniel, I may not belong to the city, but I was brought up in the good ambience of the sisters' convent. They always taught us to acknowledge with gratitude even a small favour you receive," she said categorically.

"You are right. We have to always express our gratitude. It is part of my job; my salary is paid, and the cost has been paid for the flat in which we stay."

"But we are paying EMI. The question is, are you doing this because painting for Madam Seema is also paid? Don't you feel this is a favour you are doing?" Sarah said.

"Please, Sarah, shut up; you are crossing the limit." Daniel was now angry.

"No, for five years I never said anything. Night after night you come late, work in the studio, and your worry is to make Seema Ma'am's art show successful."

"Yes, it is true; we are being paid Sarah; we are blessed."

"No, Daniel, you are sold!"

He almost slapped her. But thankfully, he quickly came to his senses and stopped himself.

"Please, Daniel, do it. I have no regrets. My sleepless nights—must be rewarded appropriately," Sarah said. He fell silent and slumped in the corner chair, totally shaken and covered his face with both hands. It has never happened before. What has come over me?

"Sarah, I am sorry; I never meant to hurt you," Daniel cried.

She went and switched on the TV and selected the "Art Show" channel.

"I didn't either. Just stating the obvious. Why does she disregard you and take advantage of you... for how much? Sara enquired.

"You're right." Daniel begged Sarah to sit beside him. "I have to be honest. From the bottom of my heart, I love her. It was a chance that God gave me when I moved to Delhi because I didn't have anyone to look up to. You are aware that I have no memories of my mum. I've never experienced the love of a mother or a sister. She quickly turned into everything for me, I'll admit. I adore you as my wife, however... Daniel broke down in tears.

"My question is simple, Daniel. In this same given situation, if I come and share with you the experience, will you be okay with that? I, too, am an orphan. The convent never told me who my parents were. The convent lifted me from the gate when I was only six days old. The question is: will you accept me if I come at midnight after working for somebody? I never doubted your integrity or love towards me."

"Please, Sarah, please. I cannot explain or express what this relationship means. But I never loved you less."

"Yes, I know, but less than Madam Seema. Why did you say that? Why did you compare me with her? I have nothing against her; she is everything to us. Why does she ignore you and not invite you to any public function? She needs you before and after, which means she doubts you and does not trust you.

"You do the painting; she will do the talking, and her work will come to the attention of the public. You may be acting innocently, but in the art fraternity, many people know who is what and your colour composition and style." Sarah expressed her displeasure.

He understood her feelings, but there was no option, and his integrity was not up for debate.

"You have a lot of misconceptions and misunderstandings," Daniel said.

"That is what you say, but I know she feels insecure!" she said, gritting her teeth.

Chapter 5

"I don't know what to say," Daniel said.

Daniel was conciously acting innocent, even though he knew he was confused. The guilt exists, and it endures. Heart of heart Seema knows her contribution is zero. But she does not want to acknowledge it in public.

"Sarah, you are staying at home, so you don't know what is all going on in the art world outside. She is not the only one. There are many.

Even senior celebrities do this. They have been sick or bedridden for years together. Some cannot even hold the brush or sit up and work. They all do the same. What is wrong with it? I am paid for my labour, and in many cases, the signature is also not done by the artist as they are not in a position to sign. Their hand is not steady," Daniel explained.

"But is it right or wrong?" Sarah said again.

"Please don't judge. I am asked by someone to do a particular style of painting; after that, what happens is none of my business. How can you expect, on all shows, to see new works by late celebrities? Even the signatures are not original. But even then those paintings are sold out."

Daniel continued by explaining how his friend Surya works with numerous up-and-coming middle-aged women and some men who are powerful and wealthy and who aspire to be recognised as artists. "Most of them are housewives and spouses of wealthy business people. These women desire to become famous overnight. They have plenty of time and money at their disposal. They want the world to know they are busy. It is a commercial assignment for us artists.

He continued by saying that all young artists, like himself, are aware but never speak up. They are paid to be quiet, so they are aware of what they are doing. However, there is no fraud or forgery because they do not copy anyone's signature.

"Matter of fact, in our college days, we did drawings and sketches for the final year students when they had to prepare their portfolios and their thesis. So we juniors had to help. Seniors will take it as a privilege, so this custom did not start today." Daniel stated, trying to justify his stand.

"If your conviction is so strong, no one can change it," Sarah replied with an air of resignation.

"Can we finish the matter here today?" he pleaded.

"I don't know, Daniel. Only time will tell. Until then, come, let us have dinner."

Dinner was finished in absolute silence, and he did not light the candle. They used to enjoy eating in the soft glow of the candlelight. But tonight, even dinner, was stressful. Sleep was eluding him. Is it anything with Seemaji, and knowing all the feelings of Sarah – Daniel had a sleepless night.

Chapter 6

At Delhi's 'Garhi Studio Campus,' groups of young artists gathered in front of the modest café under a neem tree are a common sight. The location has long been known as an art centre for emerging artists. So Surya and his pals would gather in the evenings around the famous neem tree in front of the small cafetaria on the Garhi Studio campus for a chat. The subjects were usually on what was going on in the capital's art scene. More importantly, it would focus on the less-than-savory aspects of the fraternity that people outside the fraternity were rarely aware of. Surya's bold approach was always appreciated by the young artists. He was very friendly to everyone, but he was known for his Jewish or Marwari thinking when it came to business and money.

Surya, was known for his political comments. Whenever he opens a new topic you find great energy and enthusiasm in him. All his talks go like this.

"Look, dear friends, listen to me. How do you know the economy is doing well? Check the real estate builders. If there is a boom, it means the slowdown is over. Artists are not that articulate, like politicians, who are good at convincing people, also know that all the lies they sell in public are white lies, as pure and honest. They know how to convince, give false statistics, and it is also an art. But we cannot put everyone into one category. Many believe in simple living and high thinking. We title them, honest people". He continued.

"Ours is a surviving democracy, takes time to reach bigger heights of higher standards and disciplines, and we have to be full of hope and try to be optimistic. Come on, let us call it a day, too many serious discussions. Let us stop. See you then." Surya walked off, which he always does, leaving listeners in suspense for the next round of breaking news, leaving his next discourse to the imagination of the listeners.

He had extensive interactions and communication with reputed galleries, buying houses, and he was well recognised in the art world. He would be the first to learn about what was going on in the art world.

He would coach the newbies, who would be equally happy with the pearls of wisdom that came their way.

"No charity to anyone, unless they are sick or in need of medical attention, so we must take our share of the profit. Brokers come to us for deals, but very few come as direct buyers. The buying houses have their own trusted agents. Have you not noticed — the agents come to us with a fake story?"

Surya went on to explain how an agent would pose as though he were new in the trade and only trying to help someone — to buy a work. As though he is doing a favour for someone, all lies to make fools of the artists. Usually, he would drive up in an old, battered car. His appearance would be bedraggled—an unshaven, dishevelled look. From his appearance, one would think he was not very affluent. He would be like a 'kabadi' or scrap dealer, who comes to buy waste materials. He would act all innocent, as if he did not know anything about painting, art, or the value of the paintings. Though the agent would drop some names occasionally, he would pose as if he expected the artists to educate him. But the truth is, he knows every bit about the art trade. He is an agent for a big business house. He is operating as a middleman for someone who is very wealthy and is ready to invest in the art world but does not want his name to be disclosed.

On one occasion, Surya regaled his lot of loyal admirers about the curious case of a former government museum curator who became a celebrated artist soon after he retired. Even though, people in the know were aware that he had never made a single sketch as long as he was holding his job, suddenly, post-retirement, his paintings made headlines when a top-notch business house bought them.

"Look at his 35 years of career. Pranoy Das never had a solo show; forget that; he did not even participate in a group show. Now that he has retired overnight, he is a star. How come? Here is the role of the media and art critics: they took him to such heights of fame that he himself forgot: 'Is he really the artist?' His credentials? Studied at Shanti Niketan. Nothing noteworthy happened after that. He became a government employee and spent his life pushing pens," he concluded.

Most of Surya's friends agreed. They were all aware of how retired officials of government agencies dealing with art or visual publicity are usually in a state of dilemma after retirement. Once their jobs are over, they are in a confused state of mind. Though they lead a peaceful, hassle-free life, it is a less contended one; except for guest appearances at some art shows, nothing much can add to their credentials.

They become luminaries of the art world when the media spots them at some Page 3 event. A couple of such events, and soon he will be hogging the limelight. In most cases, the media is already aware that he will be making an appearance, and the questions to be asked are also decided in advance.

For the gullible audience and newspaper readers, some tricky questions, like whether he has any regrets about not having taken active participation in any art show, nationally or internationally, are asked. Or he is asked to comment on the work of his contemporaries.

Like the questions, the answers are also prepared in advance. "We all have different goals in life. My involvement with building up this museum was, to me, very precious. In fact, that is what I wanted. All through my life, I was adding up my work. The time has come, and I'm ready to begin my journey as an artist. Soon there will be a surprise for you." Such would be the future senior celebrity who would answer the media.

Daniel, who was one of the new entrants to the gang of boys, would hang on every word that Surya spoke. This evening, his mentor Surya decided to throw light on the trick to turn black money into white through art.

"Have you not seen that all the spouses from big business houses are art collectors and gallery owners?" Surya asked.

"You mean to say they are not genuine?" said Daniel.

"Of course, they are genuine. Buying art is genuine, but if an artist has never done any serious work throughout his life in the art world, and all of a sudden his work is bought by a buyer for an enormous price, and overnight he becomes a celebrity and a national figure in the art circle, is that genuine?" said Surya.

"But how is this possible? All of these must be made-up stories," said Suresh, who had his doubts.

"Really? Made-up stories, you think? Let us say you think your work is worth Rs. 90,000. But you never sold anything in the past. So you know what you are worth, right? If someone comes and makes an offer, 'Sir, we would like to buy your work,' for you, it is a lottery. They offer you the price you quoted, and you are happy. But there is a catch." Surya, a master at another kind of art—drama—would explain things with theatrical eloquence.

"What catch?"

"The buyer does not just pay the amount quoted by the artist but pays way more than what he quotes.

"But why?" Incredulous voices ask.

"Hang on. Now hear how the game unfolds." The group waits with bated breath while Surya takes deep puffs of his cigarette.

"The agents will tell him that we are bringing your unsold work to the market. To make you sellable, we are organising media coverage. Be prepared — we have to make a market for you; it all needs money. We do not want any commission from you, and you will get your price. But we will hike the price of your work. And we will deposit the increased amount in your account. But you will return in cash the extra amount that we have given you. You will not reveal to anyone what the actual price of your work is."

A nervous titter ran through the crowd.

"The tax liability that arises from the extra payment will be borne by the buyer. The artist has nothing to lose. And in the process, both sides will make a killing!

"Invitations, inaugurations of art shows, media, interviews, and Saturday columns followed — he quickly became a national figure in the art world. When Lady Luck smiles, no one can get in the way. From the corporate world, Mrs. Leena Rastogi bought his work; the whole world knows this story. Pranoy Das's work sold for Rs. 40 lakh at the inaugural function. After a year, Leena and Pranoy painted a canvas together, which at her art show sold on the spot for Rs. 50 lakhs.

"It should be noted that 80% of Leena's collection was sold in three hours during this show." All prospective celebrities who were invited were compensated for their airfare and hotel accommodations in the city to guarantee that their presence validated the artists' authenticity. Nobody knows who bought it or to whom it was sold. All art was purchased by holding company agents."

When Surya finished, the group sat in stunned silence. Each individual is attempting to make his or her own appraisal and judgment. "Enough is enough; I must get out of this mess," Daniel thought to himself. If I become a part of this quagmire, I will also become a part of the black money printing machine. My conscience won't let me."

"How about the other cities?" "How about Mumbai or Kolkata?"

"The art worlds of Delhi and Bombay are similar. Kolkata is different. Nothing is happening in the art world in the Madras, Bangalore and Cochin marketplaces; their attention is on jewellery and saris." Surya responded.

"Our request: why don't we call the media and give them some breaking news?" Suresh chimed in excitedly.

"Are you in your right mind?" Do you recall what happened to Shovon Sarkar? Are you unaware that there was a preview of Bikas Mukherjee and that twelve pieces were to be auctioned in the UK? Shovon Sarkar, who was on the show at the time, stated unequivocally that it was not his professor's work. Tell me where he is now. He had been threatened. He doesn't even return phone calls, and he went from being a painter to becoming a photographer. "We're all small insects; they can suffocate us and there will be no trace of our whereabouts," Surya explained.

"Surya, what ever happened to Anjana Pillai?" Daniel inquired. He'd heard bizarre reports about renowned artist Anjana Pillai being duped by her own aide and associate. Surya, on the other hand, had never spoken about the occurrence.

"Nothing; it's just one of a hundred cases." Surya appeared to be hesitant, but Daniel pushed.

"Really, just for information, what went wrong?" Daniel was intrigued.

"Are you going to write or conduct research on this subject, Daniel?" If that's the case, I say no. You must practise your trade and be a seeker of truth, like Buddha was. Anyway, I can tell you what I know. You are aware that some of these women, such as Seema Ma'am, aspire to be renowned and shine in the media, huge and famous, and that the financial game is a part of that. She was invited to a get-together party at the home of a hotelier; the owner is a widow and an art collector as well. As part of the investment, they are required to display their collection on occasion. They never acquire paintings from the artist directly. Bargaining does not meet their standards; they regard it as beneath them. Anjana Pillai's work was displayed prominently at the hostess's home. But instead of being pleased she stood in shocked silence as the host welcomed her," Surya added.

Anjana Pillai, known for her unique style, was one of Delhi's star artists. A Padma Awardee, her work has found a place in the most prestigious of museums in India and abroad. And art lovers across the board follow her.

Chapter 6

It was at one of her patrons, hotelier Priya Sarin's dinner that she realised, to her utter shock that someone was copying and forging her style.

As Priya welcomed Anjana, they hugged and kissed each other's cheeks. She turned to the painting hanging in the lobby and said: "You will be happy to see your great work is one of my precious collections." Hanging on the lobby wall was one of Anjana's oils. But no, it wasn't her painting. At least she had not painted it. But even she was finding it difficult to believe that this was not her creation.

Beads of perspiration sprang up on her forehead. Her mouth felt totally dry. She stood rooted. Unable to move. "Are you okay? You are sweating so profusely," Priya asked. The host's voice cut through the buzzing in her head.

"Oh! I am fine. Coming directly from the studio. A client came while I was about to leave," Anjana replied, quickly gathering her wits about her. It was not her work; someone had copied her style with great proficiency, and someone as savvy as Priya Sarin had been hoodwinked. She would not rest until she discovered the truth and did not want to react or deny it immediately. Priya did not understand the reason for Anjana's discomfort. She presumed that her artist friend was unhappy because she had not procured the work directly from her despite being so close and having been a long-time acquaintance.

After a long silence, Anjana finally made some appreciative noises. "I am proud you have my work, and it is displayed in a prominent position in your home," she said to save the situation. As soon as Priya had gone forward to greet the next guest, she moved to the lobby and called her assistant. But Abdul Ansari did not answer.

Subject, style, colour, theme... oh, God, even composition—everything was hers. It even bore her signature. Was her memory playing tricks? Has she forgotten when she painted this one? The work is not even one year old, as the date and year are clearly written. Last year, she had not done more than 10–12 paintings, as she was mostly travelling to spend time in the US with Payal, her daughter.

Except Abdul, no one had access to her studio, and he had been with her for more than fifteen years. She could never imagine such a mistake being made by him. It is very wrong to come to a conclusion doubting the honesty of someone who was full time at her disposal. One possibility: Could someone have stolen it from her studio? Where the hell had she gone wrong? Was it the framer? It was not a question of one painting; someone was using her name, style, and even signature. In the recent past, similar frauds have happened. Fake works by Manjeet Bawa and Bikash Bhattacharya appeared in the market. In their case, it was possible, she reasoned. Both were not well for a long time, bedridden and needing constant help and assistants to help with their work. Anjana was extremely active in social circles, travelled a lot, and interacted with the media. Yes, there was one point, though: in the recent past, she had spent very little time in the studio with Abdul Ansari.

She reasoned that when we lose something at home, we normally search inside a neighbor's house first. But first, she must do a thorough investigation of her own home, where she may find some clues.

Priya came to her as usual for a chat, treating her as a special VIP guest.

"I hope you enjoyed the evening and the dinner; I am sorry I could not spend much time with you. We will catch up some other time," said Priya, a generous hostess and a very warm person.

"Sure, by all means," said Anjana. They hugged and parted, saying goodbye, and left the party a little earlier than usual instead of hanging around and making new acquaintances.

It was already past ten o'clock. Abdul could be resting or working on personal matters in his room. She chose not to make a scene or act as if she suspected him.

Abdul manages all official transactions and sends my account expenses, trip invoices, tax-related paperwork, and so on. They get along well. Who knows, if Abdul is the perpetrator, there will be no way for her to get rid of him; it will be a huge loss. Who can stop him if he copies her work style with a few modifications?

Who should be contacted next? Mr. Sandeep Arora, chartered accountant? Nah! It wouldn't be wise at this stage.

So Anjana called her daughter Payal in the US. In every difficult situation of their lives mother and daughter turned to each other.

Payal's initial reaction was one of total disbelief. Her first question was why Abdul would do such a thing, as he had never indicated his need for more money.

"That is true, darling. Not even once has he demanded or expressed displeasure about his remuneration. I do all the shopping for his wife and children whenever he goes to his native place." Anjana was not convinced she should doubt him.

"Mama, there is a possibility. Logically, it is altogether different. He gets from you approximately Rs. 1 lakh per month. Today, your one work sells for 6–8 lakhs. He is not selling the painting as his work; the signature is yours. 'Anjana Pillai', that is quite a lot. Now we have to think twice before we take one step forward. The human mind is very difficult to judge," Payal advised.

"Okay, darling, don't worry; take care. I just wanted to inform you," said Anjana.

"Yes, Mama, I am worried about you. There's no one to help us. We have to solve this problem ourselves," Payal said.

"Yes, dear, thank you. I will let you know as soon as I can figure out what is going on," said Anjana, disconnecting the call.

A widow at the age of forty-eight with one grown-up daughter—married and divorced—life had not been easy for her. It had taken her thirty-two years to reach this level in the art market; at age sixty, her work fetched Rs. 6 lakh. How can she lose her credibility? She had only one trained hand with her, Abdul Ansari. He was not just her assistant. He was her friend, and she had come to regard him as family.

She had to force him to go to his native village to see his wife and two children. Many times she requested that he bring his family to Delhi. She ensured he had all the comforts—a second-floor *barsati* with a one-room apartment—totally at his disposal. Abdul, too, is an artist. Sometimes he comes and shows her his work; he has his own style, cubism, like Professor Niren Sen. There is no comparison to his style or theme, but Sen's influence is evident. In all these years, she never went to Abdul's room and intruded on his privacy. Maybe, sitting right there on her premises, using every amenity she has provided, he is cheating her? But what would prompt Abdul to do this? If he needed money, he had her signed cheques with him. He could have withdrawn any amount. Not even on one occasion has he demanded or expressed displeasure about his remuneration.

Trust him or not, first she must take back the cheques without hurting Abdul's sentiments, even if he is innocent. One thing is certain: something has been cooking within the house; whether it is theft or fraud, only time will tell. If Abdul is the culprit, is there no way she can get rid of him? It would be a great loss. Who can stop him if he adopts her style of work with a few changes?

As she drove back home, she ran through all the possibilities of how to catch the crook. She wanted to rush home and run to her studio. But going there so late might alert Abdul. And that won't help in finding the culprit. She decided to count and tally her accounts and ledgers and check how many of her paintings were with the framer the next morning before Abdul came down. This was a nightmare. Sleep would totally elude her tonight. Anjana decided that the best way to catch the crook was to wait and watch. She could not turn to the police. That would mean a scandal of sorts, and she knew the art world and media would be only too happy to lap it up. She could always have the help of private detectives, like the one who helped with her daughter's divorce.

The next morning, as the sun crept through the French window curtains, she realised she had woken up later than usual. She looked at herself in the wall mirror, as she did every morning, and wished herself a

Chapter 6

good morning. Today, an unknown voice inside her warned her to keep watch. She smiled at herself and promised, "Yes, I will."

As she went about her morning routine, she thought over what options were open to her. Should she change the style of her work? But in that case, her identity will be lost. She had her own individuality and unique style. Sudden change or dramatic change will invite sharp criticism from the media and the public. The consequences could be in the fall in value of the work, which she took decades to build and establish.

She headed down to the lawn and, after a brief stroll, sat down for her tea, as was her custom. As she sipped her tea and flipped through the papers, she was surprised to see a picture of Priya Sarin and herself posing in front of the painting that had been causing her acid reflux since last night. That's when the idea struck her. She left the paper on top of the table. She wanted to catch Abdul off guard and see how he reacted to seeing the painting.

She had known Abdul since the time he lived in the basement of carpenter Sandeep Sharma's building in Kotla Mubarakpur, an urban village near Defence Colony. Sharma ran a small carpentry shop. It was the initiative of the art fraternity, which mostly lives in South Delhi, to help Sharma financially by giving him samples bought from abroad to make better-quality frames in Delhi. Today, Sharma is a well-known figure, not only among artists but also among politicians, parliamentarians, ministers, and bureaucrats. He had the opportunity to meet and execute works for many seniors, like M.F. Hussain and Raza, and many upcoming celebrities, Anjana being among them. She recalled how, on one or two occasions in the recent past, he had taken her work to show some clients but returned it on time. Is there any possibility he is the conduit? Would Sharma cheat her? She promoted him in his bad times, even gave him financial support, and introduced him to many of her friends.

Was Sharma the culprit? Wait, is she getting confused? If it was only a copy of her work, then someone, say Sharma, got it copied. Then the story would have been different. Here is a new work that is not even twelve months old, signed and framed in her style, and looking absolutely authentic. Was it Sharma aided by Abdul or Abdul aided by Sharma? Who was the mastermind?

Was she not pronouncing someone guilty without any evidence? She could easily check if Sharma had done the framing. He would have affixed his stamp, logo, address, telephone number, etc., as is the practice. Now Anjana was excited. The criminal was within spitting distance.

Many thoughts crowded into her mind one after the other, like the detective mind of a keen investigator. Perhaps all artists have a criminal bend of mind; they hunt for opportunities to steal ideas everywhere they can, without leaving a sign of where the concept, theme, and colours were stolen—they call it inspiration. She laughed at her wild thoughts. Am I going mad?

She looked at the table calendar and saw that she was not scheduled to go out for any programme. She could remain in the studio. Ms. Saloni Behl was joining her for tea in the evening, and some students were coming to invite her for an inauguration show at Patna College of Art.

The next day, there was an opening at Lalit Kala Academy, where she would be their chief guest. Sharma will be there; she will also phone to confirm so that she may have a casual discussion with him, which he appreciated so much, as well as the social standing that comes with talking to a star at a gala opening while silently working in the background. She was so impatient that the wait for another 36 hours felt like 36 days. She needed to remain cool and focus her mind on something else.

She decided not to break her head further and left to get ready and dressed for the day.

As she returned to her studio, she could hear the landline ringing and saw Abdul pick up the receiver. "Sir, please hold on; Ma'am is just coming in, Sir. Yes, Sir, she is very much here."

Abdul addressed someone as "Sir" three times in one breath. Quite unlike him. She was surprised—who could be the person at the other end?

"Ma'am, I could not get the full name; it is some Kumar," Abdul said as he handed over the phone. There was fear and anxiety in his voice. She answered the telephone, "Hello! Good morning. Yes, I left early from Priya's place because there was an urgent call to make." She could see Abdul Ansari's face blanch in shock as she took Priya's name. She could sense he was paying full attention to what she was saying; usually he never bothered.

"Yes, Virenderji, of course, the work everyone admired is my recent work before I left for the US. You are most welcome—yes, sure, please do. Bye," Anjana said. Being free on Sunday, they said they would love to join her for a cup of tea.

As a matter of practice. She used to share with Abdul all the discussions and details of visitors, but today she kept quiet and headed for her chair. He rushed to her just as she took her seat. He kneeled and touched her feet.

"Please forgive me. Please don't call the police, madam. I am very sorry. Sorry I cheated you and betrayed you," he cried as tears welled up in his eyes.

Even though all night she had tossed and turned and came to the conclusion that Abdul was the culprit, seeing him sobbing at her feet, she stood transfixed, unable to move.

"Oh God! What a turn of events!" Shaking herself out of her stupefaction, she picked him up by his forearm.

"Stand up, Abdul. We have to talk." Her voice was calm.

"I will confess everything, please stop IG Sir. I am ready to leave this place right now," he begged. Panic and desperation were writ large on his face. "Okay. Tell me how long you have been doing this. Who asked you, prompted you?

"I am ready to take all the blame. I do not want to blame anyone or take anybody's name," Abdul begged. "Okay, that is it, you do not want to tell the truth or name, then let the police come. You explain to them, you only understand their language." Anjana suddenly sounded very harsh.

Abdul started wailing like a child and begging for pardon. He kept repeating that he would leave Delhi never to return. And that revealing others' names would mean there would be a threat to his life. So he was ready to accept all blame and punishment on himself. Abdul was proving to be a hard nut to crack. Anjana picked up the telephone receiver and threatened to call the police which prompted him to rush yet again and catch her feet.

Recognising the time was right to strike, Anjana handed him paper and a pen and asked him to write his confession. And just as Anjana had suspected, the confession affirmed that while Abdul's role was limited to painting, it was framer Sharma who forged the signatures and dealt with the clients. As for payment, the paintings fetched about Rs. 2–3 lakhs per piece, of which Abdul got 60%. He had been painting 4-5 canvases in her style for the market for nearly 10 years.

"I did it the first time just for fun, to see how good I am at my work, and to affirm whether I can become a painter. And I showed my work to the framer, giving him a challenge to rate the work and its authenticity, and he could not make out the difference. He kept the work and sold it, and he paid me Rs. 20,000. Then it was like a trap; demand increased, and I became a slave to my guilt with no way to escape. Sharma used to give indirect threats if the work was delayed. I did it mostly when you were out of town." He went on to reveal that many of his friends were making fakes with their employer's knowledge. Of these 'copy-fraud paintings, the assistant artist gets about 20%.

Anjana knew she had the tiger by the tail. In no way could she let Abdul Ansari leave. "Listen, you are not going anywhere. You will be with me as long as I am alive." Abdul was watching her intently.

Let Sharma know I had come to know the truth; the source was not revealed, nothing more. No more assignments for him; change the agency. Get a new framer," she concluded.

As Surya narrated the events, to greenhorns Daniel and Suresh, it was like they were listening to a fictional story; never in their wildest dreams could they imagine such a thing happening in the art world.

"Big fraud is committed by big people in high places. It always goes unnoticed. So the word that applies here is mokita!"

"MOKITA?"

"A truth everybody knows but nobody speaks." Surya concluded on a serious note.

How the hell can you judge whether a work of art is genuine or authentic, especially when it is going under the hammer in the capital of a foreign country? Imagine the scenario: here in India, there was no such art market until 2000, except for some promoters, one or two corporate business houses, and some Maharajas with their foreign colonial exposure. Suddenly, there is a boom. And as far as artists are concerned, in contemporary art, only five or six names make the grade. The late Hussain, Hebber, and Raza are considered the founding fathers. Now, after their demise, who will give the stamp of authenticity? Of course, the art collectors, the gallery owner, and their genuineness are now in jeopardy and questioned.

The night was already late, and the group decided to wind up for the day. On their way back home to Sangam Vihar, Daniel was restless and troubled. He turned to Surya and said, "All that you told us today is really true? I thought artists were sensitive and idealistic, bordering on the impractical. But from what you are telling us, it seems we are happy to bluff, deceive, and con."

"Yes, Daniel welcome to the real world. There are many such cases. I only related a few."

"More such instances?"

"Yes, in some cases, the artist himself may not be at fault. Take the case of Bibek Chatterjee, a very famous contemporary artist from Kolkata. He is recognised for reintroducing realism into Indian art. In

2000, when the boom happened, he fell ill. He remained bedridden for a long time. A lot of his work was not completed. From nowhere, the so-called wife and daughter appeared on the scene. He had lost his memory and could not move. They had very little work left in his studio, and his wife became the custodian of whatever was left, including unfinished work. They started certifying and selling in the market."

"But then, from where did so much work appear in the market?" Daniel is astonished.

"The answer is in the question. The market boomed along with the liberal policy of FDI. The wife, the daughter, and some artists' sons started certifying the authenticity. 'It is my husband's, or my father's, or this is my Abba's, etc.'"

"You mean, partly, we fall in their bracket?" Daniel asked, not happy at the thought of being a scammer.

"Bracket or pocket, to an extent, we are also partly in the gang," Surya replied sarcastically.

"Not in totality; we are only reproducing or copying the work. Nowhere are we signing or endorsing the work." Daniel wanted to make sure he was not involved in any fraudulent activity.

"No, dear friend, that is not the case. Nothing wrong with copying, but there are no statistics on how many people around the world painted, copied, or collected the same work. Now comes the authenticity and certification part. Till yesterday, the only proof was that the owner has a genuine character and that his social status has always been valued. But when art became a business, big business houses entered the trade. Often, they are fooled by small players, brokers, and middlemen, from whom they collect until they make the work reach the buyer's door — a big corridor. He collects one letter from the artist or his siblings and reproduces many copies of the certificate of the original work. End of the day, who cares, unless someone wants to expose for genuine reasons — sometimes it can be blackmailing or wanting to be in the limelight?"

"Artificially created, for a genuine market," said Daniel.

"No, dear, our entire lives we will be discussing the market issue; there is no end to it. Still, we can be honest by saying copying is an art. When there's a copy of a master's work, they write 'copy' or 'reproduction'. Here, what happened is that there was an inflated market, and some houses patronised and became godfathers for some lucky artists by accident. They, through their cronies' brokers, collect most of the work by signing an agreement: 'Look, we are going to promote. You will not sell the work in the open market. We will be the sole custodian or agent of your work.'"

"For the artist, this may be a lottery. He never earned much, always lived in rented houses and flats without a proper studio to work in, what more would he want?" Daniel said.

"So the artist became a man of thousands while the investor made a few lakhs!" Surya made the point.

"How did they create the hype and popularity?" said Daniel, curious.

"Pretty simple. Catch hold of an art critic. Get it printed in the newspapers. If nothing else, give a half-page supplement. A socialite or a small-time writer becomes a writer or curator. After a good evening opening with wine and cheese, a known celebrity inaugurates the show on the opening day. A few works sold out on imaginary figures, buyers from the world of UFOs," Surya said.

"You mean the show; the exhibitor becomes the buyer, and they are the buying house. You mean a small-time average artist becomes a celebrity in the capital world within no time?" "Daniel," said Daniel, surprised.

"Industrial houses have a number of genuine and *benami* companies. They collect the work from the artist for a few thousand—I mean peanuts—and after a few months, it is resold for a few lakhs. For a little investment — marketing, publicity, event management — you have a gain of a few crores from the market. We call it white money, and some say black money," said Surya.

"I am in shock," Daniel said, showing his surprise. "Don't worry, tomorrow you may not recognise me. If you are lucky enough, one day someone may invest, or you are a good product to promote." Surya added. At times, he could be so caustic that his tongue felt like a razor.

"Surya, you have already made up your mind that I will not recognise you if I become a great artist or a celebrity," Daniel replied, trying to ignore his friend's jab.

"Please don't take it personally and become emotional. I simply made a comment."

"Oh dear, I am full. It is midnight; let us sleep," Daniel said.

He never thought that RK Restaurant's one plate of mutton biryani could induce prophecies for the future.

"Yes, Daniel, let's wind up and wait for the new sunrise."

"Good night," Daniel said.

How does one sleep after such an overload of ideas? Daniel lay on his bed, going over all Surya had revealed. You will never be in the spotlight until someone promotes you or takes an interest in you. Your luck, hard work, and efforts will continue. One must wait; while one cannot wholly agree with or approve Surya's comments, dismissing them is tough. There is a lot of truth in that because, with the exception of a few, most of the artists among them work for a living and never receive recognition in their lifetime.

Of course, there are exceptions: Picasso, Hussain, etc. But Van Gough?

Daniel required rest. He closed his eyes and switched out the light; his mind would not sleep. He tried to take a big breath. It's 1 a.m. already. He only has five hours of sleep before he has to prepare for his meeting with Madam Principal. 'Sleep, Daniel,' he murmured to himself.

Chapter 7

It was an eventful day. Daniel was not likely to forget it for a long time to come. Seema Chopra's fifth show had opened in the city. As usual, Daniel did not attend. But like every parent whose child has gone for an exam, he was on tenterhooks until he got news of how it went. For the world, it was Seema Chopra's show. He was, therefore, as it were, a little on the edge. And then he received the email, followed by the phone call. If the content of the email had left him bewildered, the call had left him stunned. It was like a high-voltage shock—a bolt from the blue!

To rewind. That evening after school, when he opened his mail box, there was an email from a school in Dubai offering him a job! Soon after, he got a call. One, Hari Krishna, informed him that Dubai International School was offering him a job. He was informed that since he was working for DIS and his resume came from known sources, they were waiving the formality of an interview.

"But I never applied for a job!" Daniel sounded almost indignant. "Presently, I am employed in a good school, and I am married, and I have my own flat that is on EMI for another eight years, and I am financially not in a position to pay the debt and leave the job." In one breath, he had confessed it all to the unknown caller.

Hari Krishna, for his part, assured him that the administrator and trustees were already aware of his situation. And since the administrator of the Dubai school had already spoken to Seema Chopra, there were no roadblocks to his appointment.

Daniel, however, was not convinced. In fact, he was quite outraged and labelled it a scam, especially because ma'am had not told him about it. "But she never said a word to me; moreover, this sort of scam is always on the internet. At the end of the day, once I leave or quit the job, I will be nowhere. Cheating is plentiful these days. I am sorry; my friends have gone through this sort of experience. Please don't misunderstand me; I just cannot believe this".

The time was 7.30 in the evening, and Sarah was in the kitchen. Before he broke the news, he wanted to make doubly sure that all the details Hari Krishna mentioned were actually in the mail. He had to verify the credibility. Maybe someone was merely playing a prank.

He quickly opened his email again. The letter was very much there, addressed to Mr. Ashok Daniel, Head of Art Department, Delhi International School.

The school's building photo was used in the top right corner as a logo. The letter ran as follows:

Dear Mr. Ashok Daniel, referring to the telephonic interview and subsequent discussion, we are pleased to appoint you to our school's art department. Your job includes making weekly visits to our other schools in Dubai for future expansion and conducting art workshops, seminars, exhibitions, etc., apart from your regular duties as head of the art department.

The letter went on to state that, besides his monthly remuneration, he would have furnished family accommodations and 30 days of annual paid vacation with to-and-fro airfare to India, including for his spouse and children. Free education for his children and all other facilities are applicable as per the school's rules and regulations. The letter was signed by the managing trustee, Mary Antony. The letter had been copied to Seema Chopra. So Ma'am was aware.

Daniel read the letter over and over again; he could not believe many of the things written in the offer letter. It was all true. There was no doubting the intent. The offer was real. There was no ambiguity left.

The question was, why did she forward his resume for a job outside the country? Does she hate me so much that she wants me as far away from her as possible? Or is it because she cares? She wants to see me prosper. Is she so selfless? Or maybe she never wanted to be associated with him for such a long time. And once she retires, then who will help her with her future shows? Not even once did anyone doubt her work, nor did the media question her authenticity.

There's no chance of hate. Considering everything he was doing for her, the principal and he were more than friends. Sometimes, he even wondered if, in some way, she could be related to him. How else would he explain the unspoken bond they shared? But how can she send me out of school? Won't she miss me? Who will help her after he goes; there are only six months left before her retirement? His mouth was dry, his throat was choked, and his eyes were wet.

There were many times when he would compare her to the make-believe image of his mother. He had often imagined what his mother would look like. Mrs. Meena Singh told him that he looked like a Keralite. So he drew up an image of his mother as a typical Malayalee lady with curly hair, with the curls flying on both sides of her forehead. In comparison, Seemaji is so different. She was almost picture-perfect. Beautiful hairstyle, no extra fat, never a single hair out of place. Each and every one of her hair strands is under her command. She always wore pastel colours; the *palloo* of her sari is so long that it almost touches the ground. Besides, she is not only charming, but she also has a strong personality!

She probably has nothing in common with my mother. Then why was he taking so much interest and time in making her shows successful? Is it because he was in awe of her? Was it because she was his boss? Was the relationship between them a mere boss-subordinate one?

He used to hear from friends who had mothers that they sacrificed anything and everything for their children. His mother's love was something he had never experienced. During his childhood as an orphan, mother remained just a noun-adjective. Is it out of motherly love that Seemaji is sending him away? Even though it would not be easy for her without him.

Is his and Ma'am's relationship that of a mother-son relationship? Or is it that of a mentor and mentee? They were both mentors and mentees at once. In art, he was the coach, but in life, she was the guide. They had fun together. They laughed, gossiped, and discussed every subject under the sun without any reservations. Over a period of time, the relationship developed to the point where there was no wall between the two. Ma'am told him very often about her relationship with the Brigadier. They had no-holds-barred conversations. He, on his part, would share even the petty quarrels he had with Sarah. Yet, they never set a bad example for society. Brigadier Rajesh or any of her children never interfered in their friendship. There was a certain passion in the relationship.

Her minor illnesses bothered and disturbed him. He remembers her having bronchitis when she arrived from the United Kingdom. The cough was awful, and she missed over 15 days of school while recovering. He came to see her every day and was always near her bed. The day she cried while holding his hand is still fresh in his mind.

"Daniel, please have a seat. Pull up a chair." He was sitting right next to her. She had his right hand in her own. Her hands were very soft and warm. She rubbed his hands and looked at his palm as if she were reading it.

She said, "Daniel, I don't know what to say or how you are related to me. Maybe in our last birth, we were born into one family, or maybe we were friends. Mother and son, husband and wife, or brother and sister. I am sure in our next birth, we will meet again."

She had tears dripping down her cheeks. He hated seeing her cry. He wiped away the tears with his left hand. She did not object. He remembered every minute of that day as if it had all happened just yesterday. She had pressed the bell by her bedside. And when the maid walked in, she asked her to bring *tulsi* tea for them both. Once again, she reached out and held his hand for a long time.

"Daniel, many times I wonder why you were not born in my family." Even though we are so close, you are so near and so dear to me, yet something is missing."

Chapter 7

Both liked *tulsi* tea. Even their choices and tastes have so much in common. Then why did she make this request to someone for a favour for his placement? Maybe there is a possibility she is also trying to find a job abroad after her retirement. So she would have planned to let him go first, and then she would follow. "It could be possible. The new developments needed clarification." He decided to prepare and answer all the questions. The situation was very puzzling. If he denies the opportunity, will she be unhappy?

He needed to know why she did it without even asking him. Had he ever expressed any desire to go abroad? She always wanted him to flourish and prosper. She made sure that once in a while, one or two of his works were sold to some of her clients for Rs. 30,000–40,000. One day, he must carve out a name for himself. The name Daniel should count for something. It should have some recall value, at least among art lovers.

Is Seemaji only trying to pay him off forever? Is she doing it out of obligation and paying for his hard work? Why was she doing this to him? He felt like crying. He could not imagine life without her. In the last two and a half years, not a single day could he recall that they had not met each other, except during her annual holidays when she went abroad. She was the pillar of his life, giving him confidence in how to dress, how to walk, and how to appear in public to speak. It was because of her that he was confident today. What may this relationship be called if it's more than just a close friend or someone you know behind the scenes? She never showed him any extra affection in front of others. She was always incredibly loving, considerate, and caring in private. Could this connection qualify as platonic or as a form of spiritual love?

Then a thought struck him. Before he speaks or clarifies, he has to make sure that he has never committed any mistake that would displease her on any occasion. His mind was replaying events with which she might have been dissatisfied in the past. He could not come up with anything that might have disappointed her. Maybe his intentions were right, but it was not necessary that the other person would have felt the same way. He needed a post-mortem of all past incidents to come to a proper conclusion.

And how do I tell Sarah? Hearing the news and the pay packet, she would jump with joy. This was indeed a breakthrough beyond imagination, but what about his feelings? His heart was aching. He had a sinking feeling in his stomach. Let the sea of events settle down before I speak to Sarah.

Occasionally, his wife did question his late-night returns, despite knowing about Seemaji's generosity. The financial stability they enjoyed today was because of Ma'am. And she was very cordial and friendly to Sarah whenever they met. "Sarah, you are great. Give him space and time to grow and establish himself. You are so mature. All his success and growth in his career are because of you. Daniel, you are lucky." Seemaji would be all praise for Sarah every time they met.

When Sarah gets to know, she will certainly say, 'You both are conspirators' for not having taken her into confidence. To clear the air, he must confess the entire sequence of events and convince her of his ignorance. But would his wife believe him?

In fact, it would be best to wait for the next sunrise. Discuss and clarify the situation and why she wanted to send him away. Was it out of love, pity, or obligation for all the services rendered? Was she rewarding him with a job offer with handsome perks? He had to speak to Ma'am; till then, no disclosure.

They ate their dinner mostly in silence. He did try to have some pointless conversation to hoodwink Sarah. And as soon as dinner was done, he feigned sleep and headed for bed. But he did not sleep. He lay there awake, pretending. If Sarah had any inkling, then he would have to answer many questions, most of which he did not have any explanation for.

In the morning, he had to meet Seemaji. To gain clarity, he needed to ask the questions that were racing through his mind. He remembered that she always wanted to write down questions before the discussion. He may ask her, "Really, do you not want me to continue here? There are six more months for you to retire. Till then, let me stay, and we will decide how you feel about my going to Dubai. Or are you also intending to go to Dubai after retirement? Do you hate me for some stupid mistake I may have committed? Which is why you want to get rid of me by providing a lucrative placement abroad?"

Despite Daniel's best efforts, his silence and tense expression since he had returned from school had given the game away. Sarah was not just worried, but suspicious. She was quite sure his anxiety was not because of their late-night argument. It was something bigger that was eating him up. However much they may quarrel or disagree on issues, they never go to sleep without making up. Tonight, things were wrong—very wrong. Sleep eluded Sarah as well. She, too, decided to wait for the sunrise. Maybe their problems will be cleared away with the rising sun.

She was always an early riser; she would wake him up. That was the way he liked it. They would sit on the bed, enjoying their black tea with lemon. Though she was a coffee drinker, she too had taken to his kind of very light tea. But this morning, things were different. The dawn had failed to clear the air. He had not waited for his tea and was already in the bathroom. The toilet door was closed. She had to take matters into her own hands. She knocked.

"Daniel, what is it? Are you upset with somebody? What is eating you?" She screamed into the gap between the door and the frame.

He did not answer. "Open or I will shout". He obeyed.

"Please wait, Sarah; I am coming out."

She could hear the water gushing out of the tap in the basin. After what seemed like an eternity, Daniel finally stepped out and almost bumped into her as she was standing with her face almost stuck to the door.

"Yes, tell me what is worrying you, Sarah." He tried to sound calm.

"Nothing! I know that, for me, there is only you and no one else. I worry only about you. There is nobody in the world to worry about me," she cried as big, fat drops of tears tumbled down her cheeks.

"Please, Sarah," he said, embracing her with both hands. She was silent and did not react as he held her head to his shoulder and stroked her neck and shoulder. As he felt her relax, he took her hand and kissed it.

"You love me?" That was Sarah.

"Yes, of course." Daniel

"Only me?" she asserted.

"Sarah, a million times I've murmured this in your ears: I love you."

"Now I want you to shout; the whole world must hear. Sarah, I love you—only you!" she demanded. He only smiled in return, bent down, and carried her to the bed. They lay in each other's arms. They had no concept of how fast the time flew that morning.

"You are late," Sarah gasped as she looked at the clock across the room.

"Yes, I am late. At least from now on, you'll never doubt me. Promise?" Daniel wanted an affirmation.

"I will doubt you every day of my life till my last breath, every hour, every second," she said with a naughty smile. He was sitting on the bed. Sarah took his face in both palms and repeated the words,

"You are only mine, only mine, and I'll love you till my last breath".

Chapter 8

Sarah watched as Daniel went around their small apartment as though he were being forced to walk. He was dragging his feet. His shoulders were drooping. He wore a forlorn expression. He looked like someone who had lost everything. She surmised that her husband was clearly upset. But what was upsetting him so much? He had not mentioned anything of late that could cause him such agony.

Tomorrow is the Hindu festival of *Rakhi,* or *Rakshabandhan*, a popular festival in North India. She knew her neighbours were busy preparing for it. Was he upset about not having any siblings? Maybe he missed having a sister—a sister to call him brother, tie the sacred thread on his wrist, and pray for his long life? Or is he simply upset because school will be closed tomorrow for *Rakhi* and he will not be seeing his favourite person in the world—Seema Chopra? A stab of jealousy pierced her heart, and she almost grimaced in response to the intangible pain. She knew Daniel loved her and that their marriage was safe.

The principal is old enough to be his mother. Yet, Sarah could not help feeling that there were three people in their marriage. She was nice to Sarah, sending her occasional gifts. But still, it was difficult for her to trust the elder woman. Is this how a daughter-in-law feels about her overbearing mother-in-law? She would never know what kind of feelings she would harbour if she had a real mother-in-law. She needed to lighten the mood in the room. Shake Daniel out of his pensive mood. She turned to Daniel and tried to crack a casual joke.

"You also want to celebrate *Rakshabandhan* just as we see in Hindi films? Want a sister to run up to you screaming, "*Bhaiya Bhaiya!*" "No. I am fortunate that there are no sisters, no brothers, and no responsibility—

nothing to give or take. If they exist at all, they are not biological relations. Sarah, as far as relationships are concerned, we are in the same boat."

"Good, it's better that way. You always wanted to promote others. I never complain; husbands promote their wives and children. Your focus was always on somebody else; you feel your life is indebted to someone; you feel obliged; nothing is wrong with that," Sarah replied.

Daniel was silent. This was not the right time to react. Furthermore, an argument would lead nowhere and to no satisfactory conclusion. Sarah had every right to be angry. His daily routine had left him no time, and he too felt guilty at times. His activities were always centred on the school and Seema Ma'am. Sarah and his friends were always there for him, but he sincerely felt that none of these people could have a deep impact on his heart. Is he being selfish?

He sat in one corner of their living room, lost in deep thought. All he could think about was Seema Ma'am and what it was about her that made him want to cling to her. Run to do her bidding? Was it because she had ensured financial stability and security? Yes, that must be the reason. No more isolation, the fear of childhood memories, or loneliness. Now he had the responsibility of looking after his wife, Sarah. His self-appraisal concluded that there was nothing wrong with what he was doing. In the given situation, he is trying to do his best. There is a lot to give and take, but a sense of responsibility and integrity always played a pivotal part in any project that he took charge of. Sarah now and then indirectly reminded him how the celebrities promoted their spouses, siblings, and children. Fortunately, she would say, we are not yet parents; otherwise, it would have been a much more serious issue.

As for Sarah, except for the sisters of the convent, who groomed her, and one or two of her roommates from her childhood, she had no one with whom to communicate. There are cases of some of her friends who never kept in touch after marriage; after they settled down, they did not want to reveal their identities to their families. Sarah, on the other hand, never denied to anyone that she had been raised by the Mothers of Charity.

Chapter 8

In many cases, there are no records of who brought them to the convent or about their parentage.

As she grew older, Sarah realised trying to obtain those details would be a futile effort because the sisters dodged any probing questions. All she was told was that, per records, an autorickshaw arrived in front of the gate around 5.30 a.m. A young lady, aged 25 to 26, expressed her desire to meet with the Mother Superior. The guard had been strictly instructed not to let anyone inside the gate until he received the 'yes' from the sisters in charge at the reception. It was the height of summer in Delhi, and the city was sweltering. The coolness of the early morning had lulled him into sleep. The lady had woken him up and stated that she needed to see the Mother Superior right away. He responded that unless the sister in charge personally comes and records the name of the visitor in the register, nobody is allowed to enter the campus.

She had a baby covered in a cotton wrap, but he could not make out if the infant was a girl or a boy. Realising the seriousness of the situation, he immediately went in to inform the sisters. But when he returned, the woman was gone. The child was lying on the reception countertop. He came out of the guard room and ran after the fleeing autorickshaw but could not stop it. He stood there, staring at the infant. He did not know what to do. He was scared he would lose his job for allowing the woman to go. He knew that, as per government rules, sisters cannot receive a child once someone accompanies the child, and all particulars must be on record. But when the infant started crying, he was left with no option but to pick up the child and hand it over to the sisters.

The guard had seen many children brought to the Home during his ten years with the Mothers of Charity. In most cases, parents behaved more responsibly and left the centre only after doing all the formalities. There were very few instances where parents left their unfortunate children at the shelter's door. These were especially those who were born differently abled or were intellectually disabled. This was the first instance of a mother leaving a child in the guard room and running away. For the Mothers of Charity, this was nothing new; they considered the baby another gift from God. If anything goes wrong with the child, the Charity has to answer to the government authority, and it will end up under legal scrutiny.

For Mothers of Charity, the new arrival was, as always, a celebration. However, as per protocol, the Mother Superior interrogated the guard to get all the detailed information needed to fulfil the government authorities' guidelines. Though they were happy to receive the child, they could not neglect the responsibility of being an institution.

The child was a female, approximately 6 or 7 days old. The guard was sure the accompanying woman was the real mother, as he saw while she was there for a few minutes that she was breast feeding the child. From her appearance and diction, he felt the woman could be either from Odisha or Jharkhand, and her age, on his assumption, would be between 23 and 25. She was speaking in Hindi, and she left behind a discharge certificate from a nursing home in Lado Sarai, South Delhi. The intention of keeping the discharge slip was that it clearly indicated the date and time of birth. Names of the parents were not mentioned. The address was eventually discovered to be fake by the sisters' source.

It was unusual. Their argument lasted more than an hour. He was watching the TV coverage to see the report of yesterday's art exhibition. Sarah was silent all through.

The silence between them continued today. Daniel was resolute, and he wasn't about to budge even an inch. He made no attempt to get up for supper. But he'd never slept on an empty stomach before. It had never happened before in Daniel's life, and he was always hungry. Who would be the first to break the silence?

Sarah believed she was right to be upset because she had not made any outrageous requests. Why was Daniel being so obstinate? What was he trying to hide from her? She reasoned that I'd be better off closing the wound. Is he going through any problems at school that he does not want to disclose? Now she was getting impatient and restless. She needed to know the truth.

Chapter 8

"Daniel, tell me, is there anything that you are feeling hesitant to disclose? Whatever the problem, I will unconditionally support you and be with you," she said.

Daniel was mentally prepared to disclose the email and offer from Dubai. Was she already aware of the contract details? Had she, by any chance, overheard the telephone conversation or seen the mail?

But before he tells Sarah, he needs to make sure first about Seemaji's intention to send him abroad and, if so, why. Seema did speak to him after the show, but she did not betray any awareness of today's development. Maybe Hari Krishna from Dubai International School had informed her before she telephoned him.

Sarah, he was sure she would agree at once; the details of the perks and terms and conditions were so attractive. The question remained: should I wait for the next day or disclose the details to Sarah now?

For the time being, he decided not to tell Sarah anything. It's best to hear from Seema first, who was waiting for his report and reviews about the TV coverage of her last show. Anyhow, he could not hide Dubai's offer from Sarah until tomorrow. The situation would turn volatile, and all that he was going to say would be just half-truths.

He expressed his views. The TV coverage was great, with lots of good words and good things being said about her. The theme she selected for the show was appreciated. The TV anchor who covered the programme spoke well about the show, and the reporter presented a good report. The talk was very cordial, with a note that the next show would have to be a little better and more focused, the subject changed, and the medium of painting could be oil on a big canvas and not acrylic.

Once again, there was no mention of the Dubai job offer. Possibly she was not aware. She might have forgotten; she may have mentioned about Daniel to someone during some seminar or meeting. Many times, people speak very highly of our colleagues, friends, and especially our near and dear ones. We recommend it out of love and even out of context.

"Some near and dear ones." He repeated the words. He needed to believe it.

It was past 11. Quite late by his standards. It was time he made up his mind. There was no reason to keep it a secret. If he hid it from Sarah any further and she learned later that he was hiding it from her, then all faith and understanding would shatter. And he does not want to become an unfaithful husband to his wife.

Then what is keeping him from disclosing this happy news to Sarah? Simple: He did not want to be away from Madam Seema, a trusted friend in every need and pillar of strength. "A better opportunity with a fourfold salary—then what is it that is eating me up?" he murmured to himself.

"Daniel, enough! I cannot hold my anguish anymore. Please tell me what's wrong. I don't want to see you like this. Did anything go wrong in school? Did you lose the job?" Sarah demanded.

"Yes, almost like that." Daniel replied instantly.

"Is it something with Madam Seema? Have you fallen in love with her?" Her voice reflected the rancour. Daniel was at a loss for words. He was finding it impossible to explain. He just kept his mouth shut.

"Listen. I am your wife. I am with you through all the ups and downs. Never worry. God has many ways to take care of us. When we got married, we never imagined we would come to a stage like this. I have immense faith in Him and in you; we will find a way." Sarah came forward and sat next to him. Her hands were shaking.

Her statement aggravated his nervousness even more. He had no right to cause her more anxiety.

"Sarah, forgive me," he began. "How do I tell you…? I got a job offer from Dubai. But I don't want to leave Delhi."

Sarah looked stunned. She sat there, dumbfounded. Then, as the import of what he had just revealed filtered through, she jumped up, kissed his forehead, and held his face in both of her hands like a mother.

Chapter 8

"At last, God has heard my prayers," Sarah said excitedly.

"You mean you were praying for this opportunity? Never once in the last five years did you say something like this," Daniel said, expressing his surprise.

"That is true. In our convent, sisters always taught us and made us believe that God always listens to silent prayers," Sarah very calmly replied.

This meant Seemaji was only a medium, and Sarah was the culprit. But why? It shows she was not happy with my earnings, late nights, and closeness to Seemaji. How do you read the mind of a woman? Was Sarah aware of his silent feelings towards Seemaji?

There were times when he would wonder why Sarah never looked really happy. Today's her smile and her expression – you feel like a hidden flora broken down from a hard rock.

But now she was genuinely smiling. Her face was radiant with joy.

"My dear, why are you in shock? A man is not a man when he doesn't know to grab an opportunity that has come to grow and bloom! An unhappy face is not a good omen. Let us thank the Lord." Sarah was now giving a piece of advice.

"You don't understand, Sarah." He could not shake off this lousy mood.

"If I don't understand, then who does? Let us now pray to the Lord to guide us on the right path to our destiny. He knows what is good for us," she said. Somewhere in her heart, she knew why he was not happy. He did not want to leave Seema Ma'am. How the hell does the woman have so much influence on him?

"Dear, who recommended you for this new assignment?" Sarah asked.

"Who? What do you mean by who? Except, Madam, who would? Did anyone ever help us in our lives? She is the only one there for us. I believe it is an endorsement of her love for us," Daniel replied.

"Well, she is retiring soon. Maybe that's why she did it. The next principal can be anybody, and new incumbents always inquire about who was loyal to the last. Then they always sideline him in the third or fourth position. Don't they? They believe one can be loyal to only one person in one's lifetime. Remember how it was in our convents? Everyone, including the CM, PM, and corporate CEOs, does the same thing. The favourite person of the last regime is always transferred. It will be a *fait accompli* situation, and you will be even sadder later when she retires... Daniel, Seemaji loves you so much. Just the way you do." Sarah gushed in one breath.

Oh God! Sarah is well aware of Ma'am's feelings towards me and mine towards her. Still, she never expressed any displeasure, except on some occasions when he returned late. Is she imagining things about my friendship with Ma'am? Does she realise it is not limited to the opportunity she has secured for me?

Sarah requested they turn in for the night as it was already rather late. From the look on her face, he knew she was already dreaming of life in a foreign country. She has enough knowledge about where one can prosper and go abroad for better prospects thanks to the news media.

On the other hand, Daniel's lack of enthusiasm was once again tormenting Sarah. Would he change his mind tomorrow? Will he refuse the offer? Seemaji herself made all these arrangements. He had no choice left. She tried to calm her excited nerves.

Like most artists and creative people, Daniel's temperament was sometimes too unpredictable. He threw tantrums and behaved eccentrically.

Sarah thought to call Seemaji and say thanks. But he may not like it, and it could lead to an unpleasant situation. She had to be careful.

Sincerely, she wanted her husband to be free from the clutches of Seema Madam. 'Can any wife stand it if her life, space, and love are to be shared by another woman?' she murmured to herself. God had heard her prayers. She crossed herself, then leaned forward and crossed Daniel's forehead.

Come sunrise, there will be a new story to begin, with a new direction. Only time will tell what path God has chosen for them. Sarah smiled and thanked Jesus once again for having heard her prayers.

Chapter 9

As usual, Daniel left home with his lunch box, carrying a fixed menu of three chapattis, one vegetable, three slices of onion, and one piece of lemon pickle. He was never deprived of breakfast. And, as for packing the lunch box, Sarah has always considered it her right and responsibility, which she has never failed to fulfil, regardless of her mood or health. The other teachers appreciated his lunch many times when they would share theirs; everyone's food was a little extra, and he too loved to share with his colleagues. Lunchtime was always a happy moment.

After the morning assembly prayers, everyone went to the classrooms. While passing through the corridor, Daniel usually made it a point, like a habit, to glance into Madam Seema's room just to wish her well before he entered his classroom. He might have missed her on one or two occasions when she was ill during the last four years of his career.

Today, he impatiently waited to meet her to get first-hand information about last night's conversation and the mail from Dubai. They may have forwarded a copy to her, or she could have had the information beforehand. He thought she should call or convey the news to him before he went to her room and disclosed the mail details and the developments in his house.

Why did he feel apathetic today, when it had always been his practice, like a foolish child, to go to her at break time and share all the good and bad news of his happiness and sorrows of the previous day? He kept no secrets from her. He would admit to even minor fights at home with Sarah and would get a scolding followed by good counselling to help him understand and overcome family problems. She was an excellent counsellor, mother, mother-in-law, sister, principal, colleague, and friend;

he relied on her for everything. She has been and will continue to be his pillar of strength.

Instead of waiting for the attendant to come and invite him to accompany him to the principal's room, he decided to wait until 11.30 a.m., the midmorning break. He ate breakfast, but his stomach was still burning. Daniel ate more when he was worried. He had another two and a half hours until lunchtime.

He had never once offended her in the past and was always very careful not to enter her room without prior permission. When she is in a meeting, the 'Lakshman Rekha' is never to be breached. Pretending as if he were going to the restroom, he left the classroom for a few minutes.

Sometimes, he would meet her on the way while she was on her surprise visits to the classes. He walked fast and took a chance, although he knew he ought not to. He needed more time to explain to her, as he could not tell everything in a few minutes. In the meantime, suppose someone enters her office and all the efforts are sabotaged. He does not want to do a premeditated talk; everything should be spontaneous and natural.

He saw her leaving some parents at the door, who might be VIP guests or some other very important people. She would never accompany nonentities to the door.

Daniel could tell from a distance that they were very important people. She was looking majestic in 'Her Highness's" virginal white sari with a sky blue border, always with her ballpoint pen carried in her right palm, rubbing and rolling. Nothing can change overnight; it seems his offer of an appointment with the Dubai School and his leaving DIS are not very important for her. Had she taken it very seriously, she would have called him by now. There can only be two conclusions. One, she may not be aware, or they may not have informed her.

Second, it is in no way very important. Daniel could be wrong, but his Ma'am could never be indifferent to him. Unnecessarily, his mind is straying into the wilderness. He made it a habit to try to attract her attention whenever he walked through the passage. However busy she may be, she would send the attendant to find out what happened to him, and this experience had never failed in the past. She knew Daniel was just like a child; she was quite aware of his pulse.

He dashed into his classroom, expecting the attendant to arrive at any moment with a note from her. He kept the table clean and he took steps to ensure that every student was fully involved and had enough classwork; even if the meeting was going to be a touch lengthy, the class would maintain discipline.

However, nothing happened. He assumed she was avoiding him on purpose. He resolved to wait the two hours before lunch break and then go into her office, knowing that he had that liberty and privilege and that no one could stop him. Daniel sat at his desk, took out his small pocket diary, and jotted down all of the points he had mentally prepared. He knew if he had the note in front of him, he would not forget or become distracted.

He considered taking a printout of the message delivered from Dubai and placing it on her table. He wanted to tell her that he received a call from the Dubai school informing that Madam Seema had recommended him for a position in their school. But he decided against it because it would appear rude and obnoxious. He'd have to wait unless she specifically requested it. Should he just speak to her casually and let her start the conversation? 'Daniel, tell me how everything is?' she used to enquire. Sarah?" The same dialogue every time. It is likely to be the same today as well.

He looked at the clock: 30 minutes more for lunch. Which meant another 30 minutes of nerve-wracking waiting before he could go and see her, unless she called him first. It was as if time was crawling today. His stomach was screaming for food. He needed to get a hold of his jangled nerves. Calm down, he told himself. Just count your blessings. There was a time when he would worry about getting a permanent job and owning a flat; now he has everything and exceptional freedom to work more than an art teacher. Even while he spoke to himself, he was paying close attention to every footstep in the corridor, hoping to figure out who was approaching based on the sound of the footsteps.

Try as he might, he was unable to get his mind away from the question that had plagued him since he received the apocalyptic call from Dubai. Why did she do it? Does she not love him? He has done everything, even sacrificing his own identity, for her artistic career and exposure to the art world. For him, she is his most trusted friend and well-wisher. Is he not the same for her? She had done her share of helping at the time of his need to get a job and a loan for a house, for which he has remained grateful to this day. For seven years of his career and stay in Delhi, he received no recognition as an artist in the art world, and he is only known as an art teacher, nothing more.

Many of his contemporaries are established artists, with the majority not even employed by any organisation or institution. Is there any reason for any analytical study now about the appointment for a change of job, place, and respectful assignment in a foreign country? As far as his identity is concerned, he was hardly known to anyone in the art world until he reached Delhi. He was an orphan, abandoned by his parents and brought up by a Christian orphanage, through whose goodness he has today become a fully blossoming art teacher. Once he struggled for survival; today he is looking for fame and success. Why are there all these conflicts of interest now?

What should he do? A decision must be made before he meets her. He realises that Dubai is a great opportunity that he must accept and move forward with. Yet, how can he leave Delhi, or rather, Seemaji? Is it really love, or is it interdependency turned into love? But who is in love here? He was sure that without her knowledge and recommendation, it would never have happened.

Maybe he is in love with Madam Seema, which is not allowing him to detach himself from her. Can it be because he has been deprived of love from birth, or is he a man looking for dependency and emotional support? All through his childhood, the men in his institution seldom had an opportunity to interact with the opposite sex, except with the mathematics teacher. But why are all these thoughts haunting him today? He married the woman he wanted, or was it simply his hunger to meet a girl, and his desire was fulfilled by marrying Sarah?

Sometimes he felt that if he had not met Sarah, he might have remained unmarried until he was established and had become a famous artist. He had no regrets about leaving Lucknow because, today, Delhi had given him a different image and changed his outlook towards the world. While he studied art, his aspiration was to become an artist; that was his only goal, but now he is a school teacher. He had met many artists known and renowned in the capital, and the stories were different; his perception totally changed. As an artist, he realised he was a creative person, and his work in the art world added value to his wealth. Art fascinated him, and he could paint all his life. He is untiring and has great aspirations and an appetite for a better life. Money can add value to his life. Richness is not an issue but a comfort zone where he can work without fear, a space for fame, respect, and status in society. He began to believe in himself. If he had done something in the past, whether he wanted to or didn't want to, whether it was ethical or not, he did it with conviction, even if the intention was still unclear.

No more waiting for the lunch break; he jumped up to go and meet Seema. As it was, his hunger had doubled. He could not control himself any longer. But then again, sanity prevailed, and he sank back into his chair.

"Daniel, cool down. Let her call."

Again, the torment began. His mind went into overdrive, trying to find the reason that pushed her to take this step. Why did she want to get rid of him? Had she started thinking he was a liability? In the latest review of her last show, she might have gotten some feedback from her trusted friends. Someone might have made a negative comment: "Nothing new in her work; old wine in a new bottle."

It was about lunchtime when he received a call from Surya. "Hello, *dost*! You're a *chupa rustam*! You have won a lottery! You are leaving the job and going abroad?" Surya asked.

Daniel winced. His good friend had just rubbed salt on his raw wound.

"Who told you?" Daniel asked.

"Dear friend, that is not important. Is it correct or not? Since we met almost seven years ago, there has never been a wall between us; there are no secrets. Then why have you hidden this happy news from me?" He asked, his voice tinged with sadness.

Daniel did not answer.

"Hi, are you listening? Why are you keeping quiet? It is such great news. We are looking for a treat. If not, we will all arrange the same for you," Surya said excitedly.

"Surya, trust me; only last night I got the mail, followed by a telephone call from Dubai. I was in utter shock, so much so that Sarah and I had a fight. I didn't know how to unfold the drama. I have yet to make up my mind, and I have not seen my boss," Daniel replied very coolly.

"Listen, she will do anything for you; don't worry. She is a large-hearted person and will never stand in your way," asserted Surya.

"Please listen; how do I explain to you that I am no one in this game?" Daniel said.

"You and I know this much: that after six months, the school year ends, and then soon after, she is also going to retire," Surya completed the sentence.

"What have I got to do with it? Listen, the Dubai guy said my reference was given by Seema Chopra. They have given me the choice to join at the year's end. They are waiting for my written acceptance," Daniel said.

"What is to stop you? Everything is clear; the path is clear; get ready and proceed," Surya said.

"Surya, don't misunderstand me. I will meet you in the studio after school."

Daniel felt dejected and decided to go to him and explain in person.

"Dear, there is nothing new; every day we meet in the studio," Surya said.

"Yes, I meant the same," explained Daniel.

Surya's call only compounded his confusion. There is only one source for Surya's information, which means she has told him everything. She may have needed a change without hurting him. She does not have the time to call him, but she has enough time to tell his friend Surya. Wow! He chastised himself for having invested so much in this relationship. Then again, he told himself that now was not the time to draw any conclusions. He has so much to lose: his name, status, and job. Let her reveal the truth about the developments she started.

Once again, he made up his mind to go confront her and yet again decided against it. He stayed for a while in his chair and pretended that he was busy evaluating the progress of the students. He chose to pass the time by pondering over what might have overstated about his position, forgetting that he is one among the school's eighty-two working staff members. The space and position she has provided are special and one-of-a-kind, and he has thoroughly appreciated them. Her confidence and trust in him, as well as all the other benefits—perhaps she expected him to do the paintings for an exchange. Nothing exceptional, many of his friends had been doing this all through their lives for livelyhood.

Then why is he brooding and restless? At least she has obliged with a better position in a reputed school and a new life for him to be happier and more settled. There is no place for his overwhelming emotions or sentiments. Everything is done in order; there is no reason for frustration, and he must be calm. What he has done may be done by another artist who is more accomplished and famous. Surya is another helping hand or lucky person she will use till she climbs another step in her quest for fame.

'Yes, Sarah, you are wise. We must leave this place at the earliest possible time without any sadness,' he said to himself with an air of resignation. So much for love! In the afternoon, the students went to the ground to play football. There is so much silence in the classroom. Yet when the peon came in to give him a folded and stapled slip, he did not hear him. It is very clearly from Seemaji. It is nothing unusual and quite the normal routine that, before anything, a confidential message must be conveyed in writing. He quickly opened it.

"Dear Daniel, You might have received the job offer by mail and are making all preparations accordingly." It was simply marked L, which stood for love. He kept the slip on the table and shut his eyes. This is the greatest blow he has received in his life in recent memory. He needs time to reconcile himself to it. He read the contents over and over again.

She had finally broken her silence, and soon she called on his mobile and said, "Rajesh went trekking yesterday for a week in the Himalayas. You will be joining me for dinner. Tell Sarah to have her dinner and that you will be late. And please cancel your going to the studio today."

Although it has happened many times before, this is the first time she sounded as if she were really alone. For him, going home late was nothing unusual. She knew going to the studio was a ritual for him. It was important to keep himself updated on the recent exhibitions and happenings in different galleries, and the visit to the studio gave him all the news. From her words, it was clear that she wanted to disclose and discuss all the news in person.

'Thank you, ma'am; I too want to meet you alone once; it may be our last meeting.' All of his emotions sprang to the surface, as he had feared; he sensed the impending storm.

He was restless, and he spoke to Sarah, saying he was going to the studio as usual and that he would be late.

Her reply was very casual when she asked, "Did Madam call you and say anything about the job offer?"

"I will meet her after class. This is a serious subject and should be discussed in person with more time," he replied, so that Sarah would not feel that he did not want to leave the job for a better one.

In spite of Seemaji's order, he decided to go to the studio, as a meeting with Surya before meeting Seemaji was of utmost importance. He planned to leave school a bit early rather than wait until the end of the day. He wanted to have enough time on his hands to talk to his friend. And, instead of opening the discussion and asking for details, it would be best if Surya started the topic. There would be no time to go home and freshen up before proceeding with the dinner. Besides, if he went home, he would have to answer Sarah's many questions. It would be best to go to Ma'am's directly after meeting Surya.

As he walked into the studio, old memories came flooding back. Nostalgia got the better of him. He had a feeling everything was going to end at this very moment. By leaving this space, he may lose not just too many good memories but also an important part of his life. He looked around at the partly broken stools and benches; nothing was in order except the canvases and stretchers, and the easel stood where he had left it in the corner.

Surya was waiting with a packet of sweets to welcome him.

"Arre, *bhai*, why are you sad?"

"Yes, I am sad. How do I explain it to you?"

"You are going with Sarah *Bhabhi*. Why the hell are you feeling lost?"

"Why don't you understand that I worked and lived here for six years?"

"True remeber you lived in Lucknow for 23 years. Listen, I've been here for eleven years and have done a lot of work and met a lot of celebrities and their friends—both in front of the curtain and behind the scenes. I have made financial gains, but I will never be able to make in five years what you are being offered as monthly perks in Dubai. Name and fame are all money games."

Daniel kept his silence and let him speak. Already the water is boiling in the kettle, ready for their green tea.

"Listen, I am not one to pressurise you."

"Please don't say that. Since we met, I have never taken a decision without seeking your opinion. Today I came here early to get your opinion and hear your last word on whether the decision to quit the job is right or wrong."

Surya stood up and took a couple of ceramic cups, slowly poured the hot water into each, and then dipped the tea bags.

No words were exchanged, and there was a deep silence.

When Surya finally spoke, his tone was very matter-of-fact and deliberately casual.

"Take it easy, mentally prepare yourself for the future assignment, clean all your brushes, and take stock of the materials, canvases, and paintings so you can get a fair idea of what is in our stock of unfinished work."

Daniel was suspicious of how he had learned all the specifics of his job offer, including its perks and location. How else would he know if Seemaji had not conveyed to him all the contents of the appointment? There is no point in asking until he opens the topic.

"How has *Bhabhiji* reacted? Is she happy?" Surya asked.

Daniel nodded in reply.

"Dear friend, it is important to get a job with family accommodation and all perks, including travel fares. Madam has done a good job before she retires. With only six months to go, it shows how much you mean to her. No one does what she has done; for all the service you have given her, she feels obliged and has acknowledged it. It is her greatness. In this day and age and in our field, no one wants to accept or recognise anyone's merit, especially in the artists' fraternity," Surya said. "Go home, give all the happy news to my *Bhabhi*. We are all coming for a dinner treat once your date of departure is decided."

Daniel took a deep breath, relieved that Seemaji had not informed Surya about the dinner today.

As he left the studio, a question struck him. Why had Seemaji not informed Surya about the dinner tonight? Also, why didn't Surya even once mention that Seemaji had conveyed the news of the job offer? How is the meeting going to be, as there will be so much time to spend together at the dinner table? She is a real host, a 'party person'. Every month she has social gatherings of VIPs, socialites, and elite ladies with drinks, dancing, and dinner nights. He is always there at arm's length, as a staff member from her school, not as an artist, which she has always been hesitant to disclose. In private, she calls him "D." She always introduced him to her guests as "Mr. Daniel, our most dedicated teacher." Never anything more. Never as her friend. In private, it was a different story. She was always affectionate and spoke loving words. He didn't seem to mind, for he too had a hidden motive. He had his own selfish reasons for bearing all this. In school, it is a privilege to be the principal's special person, a unique position among students and staff. Though she never overtly acknowledged him in public and tried to keep him at a distance, he was sure the school was aware of his proximity to her. He had no idea as to what extent others gossiped behind them, and if so, it did not matter. At the core of his being, he loved the position he was in.

Realisation comes very late with experience. She knows very well 'where to fix whom'," and the whole school knows about it. But Daniel was the only one who had the privilege of being a part of her household, especially at social gatherings. His role was a little better than that of hotel bearers and bar attendants: a silent observer whose role was to be vigilant and report to her that everything was going well at the party and everybody was enjoying themselves. She needed feedback, like a special confidential report, on the following day. Like a child, she would ask who was with whom and who spent more time with whom.

He also had the additional duty of doubling as an in-house photographer. She was very particular that he made sure she was in every frame as she fleeted around from one guest to the other, enjoying the presence, nearness, and fondness of one and all.

"One last word, Daniel, how is Rajesh?" "You know after his third drink he will go out of sense," Seemaji used to ask during every party.

"Oh no, ma'am, he was absolutely fine," Daniel would reply.

"Daniel, that I know, but you do understand what I mean and how he behaves with ladies," Seemaji would say.

She was always eager to see the photographs Daniel had taken, which he shared after seeing her smile and wink at him.

"You are very naughty. Yes, it is exactly what I wanted. Thanks, Daniel." Seemaji expressed her happiness.

He could only smile. It is a sort of balancing act. She is very caring with every guest, hugging and kissing them. She would make sure Brigadier Rajesh is equally important at social gatherings. It is all a game that happens in high-class, elite homes. He observed that she rarely invited the same guest twice. Sometimes, Daniel felt jealous of her closeness and the love and affection she showered on her short-lived friends at the one-time party.

Chapter 10

He reached her home at the said time, and the watchman opened the gate as the three-wheeled autorickshaw dropped him outside. She always appreciated punctuality, and he was ahead of schedule, arriving ten minutes earlier than the scheduled time of 7.30 p.m. He walked through the driveway, the pathway on both sides lit against the early beginning of the winter darkness on the lawn. Calmness and silence prevailed on the green lawn and surroundings, and there was no voice coming from inside the house. Usually, her maid or Rajesh came to the door when he pressed the bell on the porch of their newly bought farmhouse in Chhattarpur. Maybe the maid is in the kitchen, preparing dinner.

"Hello, Ma'am," he said as he heard her voice at a distance.

"Daniel, come in. I am in the kitchen, preparing dinner. The door is open," she answered.

He removed his shoes on the veranda and walked in wearing the cotton house sandals that were kept by the door.

"Come straight into the kitchen. Today, you are going to help me prepare dinner. The maid and her husband are on leave for two days as her mother is very ill, and I didn't want to stop them. You are not a guest to me but part of the family," Seemaji said.

"Of course! Tell me how I can help."

"No help is needed; we will cook together: very simple baked fish and boiled vegetables. The toast and soup are ready to serve; the kebabs will have to be grilled. You can have red wine, beer, or scotch."

"Ma'am, I prefer only white wine, but the choice is yours."

"I know you like my choice. Bring some cheese and slice it. For the wine, open the fridge. In the meantime, I will grill the kebabs."

She was behaving as though nothing had happened; everything was as it was in the past.

"Would you like to watch TV or hear music?"

"No TV, Ma'am. If you like, we can put on Ravi Shankar's sitar recital, 'Rajkhamaj'." While he drifted off towards the music system, she quickly put the kebabs on the grill.

Daniel opened the bottle of wine and poured one glass and her choice of Scotch in another glass with two ice cubes, just the way she liked it.

"I know you are hungry and have not gone home, so I decided not to waste time cooking; all the items are ready to serve."

They moved into the dining hall. She lit two candles while standing in the graceful ornamental candelabrum. The mood was sombre, though Seemaji was trying to sound peppy. Daniel tried not to look doleful. He knew he had to keep up his appearance, though he was dying to ask all the questions that had been tearing him apart. But, displaying exemplary self-control, he maintained a calm demeanour. Let her speak first and let the breaking news come from the anchor, the newsmaker.

"Daniel, just give me fifteen minutes to change my dress. I needed to freshen up as I was busy in the kitchen." As she rushed to the bedroom, he realised she was still wearing the same sari that she had worn to school.

"OK, Ma'am, take your time. I am not in a hurry," Daniel agreed.

He sat there, counting the fond moments they had spent together. He decided he would not use words to hurt her, as she had extended a very cordial and affectionate welcome. He shut his eyes and decided to meditate. Let her take her own time, she is a well dressed woman with ethics and etiquette fitting for all occasions. He could hear the bathroom door open. But there was one question on his mind, which he decided to ask: whether she liked it or not.

"Ma'am, you told everything to my friend Surya beforehand, why not to me?" The question was legitimate. He knew why it hurt so much that she preferred telling Surya than him, and more importantly, when she was choosing to send him away. Sitting there in her dining room, surrounded by everything that carried her stamp Seemaji, the truth hit him. He was in love with her. He would be a liar if he denied it anymore.

What is all this love about? She is a married woman, much older than him, with grown-up children nearly his age. He was a man of thirty who is happily married. He was deep in thought, trying to battle his inner demons. He didn't hear the footsteps when she came in.

"Daniel, are you tired? Sleepy?" she affectionately asked.

"No, Ma'am, I was just listening to the music," Daniel said.

"Good, come, let us have our drinks."

After gathering up the wine and scotch glasses, she moved on to the table. They sat across from each other. When they were together, he had seen her and the Brigadier enjoying their evening drinks at the same table. "Let us raise a toast to our happiness and the future of a long-lasting friendship." They said, "Cheers." She took her first sip.

"Ma'am, you look so beautiful; I've never seen you so composed and poised," Daniel remarked.

"You mean you've never seen me like this before?" she asked.

"Yes, Ma'am, and that too in a pink gown; you look gorgeous," said Daniel.

She rose from her seat, walked over to him, and kissed him on both cheeks.

Then she turned and walked towards the door and bolted it, pulled the curtains, and came back and sat across to him. She changed the music, humming 'Silent Night'. She took his hand to dance. Both their heads rested on each other's shoulders.

"I love you," Daniel said.

"Me too," Seema responded.

"I've waited years to say these words."

"Me too. Why didn't you ever tell me?" Seemaji said.

Daniel did not reply.

They each went to get a second drink. But neither of them appeared to be in a hurry.

"When do you want to go?" she asked.

"I never wanted to go," he replied.

"You silly, I'm asking when you want to go home," she laughed.

"Never," he said again.

"You love me so much?" she asked.

"Yes."

"From when?"

"The day we met."

There was a deep silence.

"I never had the guts and courage to open my heart." That was all he could say.

"Daniel, I am aware of your deep appreciation of everything I do, right or wrong. You know very well that I am much older than you, married, and have grown-up children about to marry," she said.

"This is all true. I never demanded anything from you; I just always wanted to be near you and feel the closeness—a feeling I am not able to explain. I love to be in your vicinity and get a feeling of security," Daniel expressed his emotions.

She is a teacher and a principal. And she was a student of psychology. She understood human behaviour, which is why she was so successful. What he was saying is right. A child deprived of his mother's care and with no father is brought up in an orphanage at the adolescent stage. Though what Daniel is saying is correct, she has her own limitations. She is aware of the future consequences and also understands his state of mind.

The option she decided to take could not have been better. She had a special liking, a bond—call it love or affection— with this boy. She had a happy childhood. Her youth was also good. Then what is she missing? From her experience with her husband, Rajesh's attitude towards her, his aloofness, many a time made her feel they were more separated than together. They were like two people staying under one roof, but their likes and dislikes were major. Life is all about adjustment, so long as you have your own space to live and explore.

Daniel is different; she always liked his presence. He is a compassionate, caring young man—a man you can trust at any time for any need. She always felt he was family. Where was she going to stop? When she had a mild illness or fever, or when he visited her home, his conduct didn't seem like that of an outsider. Brig. Rajesh too had a soft corner for him, except for one occasion when he expressed displeasure at his frequent visits to their home. He later realised that without Daniel's help, she would not have been able to make her mark in the art world. In her innermost heart, she knew her decision to send him to her school was a cruel thing to have done. It had been troubling her for a long time. There was not much choice left for her except to give him a better opportunity elsewhere.

She is going to retire within a period of six to eight months. A hard decision had to be taken. Though it is painful, there is no other option, and it must be to the benefit of both of them. As a brigadier's wife, mother of two children, and principal of an institution, she thought his presence and nearness might lead to scandal. Is that the only reason she wants him away from Delhi? No, she, too, needs an upgrade in order to survive in the art world and retain her social image. It took her nearly four years to establish herself as an artist today. To continue making headlines, she must modify the style and medium of her work.

At this moment, when they are alone, it is the right time, she thought, to discuss with him the step she has taken. He may ask, "Why?" She is feeling sad for Daniel. He looked shaken, much like someone who has lost everything in life. It was a good decision that she had informed Surya, their common friend, just to take the edge off the surprise.

Seema was likewise anxious. She would occasionally leave the Scotch on the table, close her eyes, and wipe her brow with both hands. Daniel was aware of her stress level and emotions. He was aware that she performs the same exercise in any tense scenario. He couldn't help himself; he rose up, leaving the wine glass on the table, and stepped behind her chair.

He requested, "Ma'am, shut your eyes." He took her hands, pulled both her arms down to her sides, and started massaging her shoulder. Seeing her relax, he pressed the nape of her neck and then her forehead. Seema did not object. Daniel's massage reminded her of her mother and the way she oiled her body and hair during her teenage years.

"Relax. I am good at acupressure. In our hostel, for minor illnesses, they never took us to doctors." The more he pressed, the more she relaxed.

Daniel was so confused from the time he walked into the house. This was his last chance to express his deep affection for her. "Ma'am, just finish your drink."

But she didn't listen to him and stood up to go to the kitchen to microwave the food that was ready to serve.

She said, "Are you hungry?"

"No, it's too early. Relax. I'll do it. You appear exhausted."

Even at parties, she rarely drinks a second glass of scotch unless she is agitated.

"You go lie down for a few minutes."

He escorted her to her bed. It didn't matter that she was dressed in her nightgown; they'd known each other for almost six years and had grown close.

The feelings of trust, compassion, and love for each other are undefined.

"Daniel, I am feeling so tired, and fatigue has set in," she said, her voice sounding weak.

"Not to worry, just lie upside down." Pandit Ravi Shankar's sitar continued to softly play in the background.

He sat on the side of the bed and started pressing her shoulder down on her lower back and calf muscles. She started feeling sleepy after a few minutes. He slowly turned her body to face him so that he could apply pressure to her arms and the pressure points of her feet. She was half asleep. He stood up, straightened her head, and pulled her hair to the sides. She was looking so beautiful; the nightgown had partly slipped to both sides. He sat by her feet. When he pressed the thumb of her foot, she moaned,

"It's hurting."

"Your shoulder is very stiff and frozen. You seem to be under a lot of stress," the therapist in him said.

She did not reply. He pressed both her arms, and last of all, he pressed her forehead. His breath was so hot. A drop of sweat fell from his forehead onto her face. She grasped his hands and just kissed them. He kissed her forehead and eyebrows.

"Sit by my side. Be with me till I say so," she said.

Slowly, he lay down by her side. He was very calm and relaxed. Though it could be equated to an incestuous moment, he could not resist. She did not stop him either. They became one body and soul.

"Don't leave me now," she said.

"I never wanted to," Daniel responded.

Both were quiet. Words have no meaning when two souls meet. It was an emotionally intense connection, the likes of which both had never experienced before. Time stood still. It was only when the clock on the wall chimed that Seema disentangled herself, saying, "It's 10. Sarah may not sleep till you reach home."

"She knows I will not be back without seeing you."

She realised the gravity of his last words. It was like an unopened envelope, the contents of which are known.

It was moment. 'MOKITA,' The truth everybody knows it, but nobody speaks.

Sarah already knew about the job offer and the message from Dubai. Daniel's main reason to visit Seemaji was to discuss and clarify everything, but the situation turned out to be rather different. One of heartbreak. They both sat down for dinner, and for some time they did not speak.

"Daniel, I know what is going through your mind—the job offer and its details. You could have asked many times why I initiated it," she said.

Daniel stayed deafeningly silent. She began telling him about his employment offer from the Dubai school. She went into great detail, including how she met the principal of Dubai International School two years ago at a faculty recruiting interview in Delhi. The two principals became fast friends. Seema, as Principal of DIS, was unable to provide any formal service to other institution. So she had to keep it a secret and couldn't even tell him.

"You may even ask why I told Surya, your dear friend, beforehand. As a woman and a mother, I very well understand your feelings towards me. Let it not be a surprise to you; it is very difficult for both of us to continue together. Moreover, as I am the older one, I decided to take the call. I've said a lot of things, and you haven't said anything," she uttered.

"I am dumbfounded and numb. In my world, you are everything in terms of faith and thought. You've given me so much freedom, compassion, camaraderie, and love that I don't know what else I could ask for. You gave me everything simply by understanding my requirements. 'A mother's care' meant more than anyone could have expected in this birth."

They finished their dinner. There was total silence in the room. It was like they were in a vacuum. It was time to part. He knew it might be his last visit. He sensed she needed to say something but was too emotionally overwhelmed to do so.

He broke the silence, saying, "Ma'am, tell me when I must…"

He choked; overcome with emotion, he could not complete the sentence. She came near him, put both her hands on his shoulder, wiped the tears from his eyes, and kissed his cheeks.

"Daniel, you will be away from me, but no one can take away your memories from my heart till my last breath,

Seema softly cried.

She kissed him again. This time on his lips. Daniel realised this was her parting kiss. Hand in hand, they both moved slowly towards the main door. She opened it for him and pressed the bell to call her driver. Before he got into the car, he asked, "Ma'am, when must I leave?"

"No date has been fixed; I will tell you tomorrow."

She took his left hand and rubbed it with her right hand till the headlights of the car blinked. The car came to the portico, and soon the headlights were switched off. A moment of darkness enveloped them. The driver opened the door, and Daniel got into the back seat and, sliding the window down, said,

"Bye, Ma'am."

"Bye Daniel."

As the car started, he felt she heard him calling out his name, 'Daniel' while she waved him off. It may be his last visit to her home, and they may not meet each other again at this place. He slumped back in the car. A dull ache was gnawing at his insides. As he neared home, thoughts of what Sarah would be waiting to hear about the outcome of the meeting started plaguing him. He may have to resort to telling lies to cope with her anxiety and eagerness. 'Did you say thanks to her for her generosity in helping us get a new opportunity? When do we have to go? What else did you discuss? Did she say anything about the balance of the house loan?' These are the anticipated questions. He braced himself to answer the questions arising out of his anxiety, anger, and sleepless nights.

Where did his guts fail? Is it love or selfish existentialism? There was an undefined bond beyond words and imagination that existed between both of them. It occurred to him that it seemed like the settling of an account of some previous birth, 'karma'. She is a married woman, a mother, of high social status, and more than that, a Principal for 1,800 students. His expectations and demands were not reflected virtually in his body language, which she would have avoided, discouraged, and given him space equal to any other staff member at the beginning. What stopped her—there or where?

They had both reached a stage of their relationship that had grown to the extent that they longed for a feeling of togetherness. Now the curtain has fallen on the stage. The new sunrise will bring a new horizon for both of them. The past will become a bleak memory.

At this moment, how do I face Sarah? Where do I begin to answer her eagerness to know about the meeting? 'Have you changed your mind after meeting her?' Sarah very well understands that he would rather continue at the school, though he never reveals his feelings. If Daniel commits to leaving the school, Sarah will achieve financial freedom, as any woman would demand and expect. Besides, he will be back and will only belong to her. She is right; it is justice. The fantasy and myth of love will remain an untold story. He called her, as it was much simpler than keeping her in suspense and waiting.

"Sarah, our departure to Dubai is final. My farewell from school will happen after Ma'am informs us of the due date to leave. Everything went very well, and we are leaving Delhi soon. All your prayers are heard. I'm on my way and will arrive in half an hour."

This day and night may be the most loving and happy for Sarah and for him."

There was total silence at the other end.

"Sarah, love, what happened?" Why are you silent?"

"Everything is okay. I was worried you might have declined the offer. I know you are upset about leaving school, Ma'am."

"Oh, no, please, I am okay. I took the decision, gave the final word, and told her thanks for her generosity and for all the help she has given to us," Daniel said.

"Thanks be to the Lord," Sarah concluded.

He reached home. It was as expected; Sarah was there with open doors to welcome him as a war hero returned with glory. A war fought in the mind. She removed his shoulder bag and asked him to take a shower.

"I have not eaten dinner. You smell like paint. You were in the studio?" Sarah asked.

He was about to say no, then quickly caught himself. He smelled of perfume mixed with alcohol. Sarah didn't make any further comments. She simply repeated,

"Take a shower." Sarah, you are a great woman. Knowing all my weaknesses, you still accepted me and forgave my mistakes. You are not a wife; no one in the world would forgive anyone, however grievous the fault may be. Except a mother, no one can do it. I am fortunate. As he stood under the spray of water, he felt the pain of the last few days wash away. A turbulent day had come to an end.

"I only live for you, only for you, Sarah." A new chapter in our lives is about to begin. A new sky will open up, and we will soon reach a new shore.

The fulfilment of an individual's dreams and expectations to suit the nature of their own selfish needs—that's what life comes down to. It was true for him, Sarah, and Seemaji. Everyone had their own individualistic needs to be fulfilled. Subconsciously, he was aching to achieve higher heights, the "awakening' of an artist as a painter. It was not sheer survival; this was a different game, and he had to play differently to win. Daniel, the orphan, had many dreams and expectations that he hoped to one day fulfil.

Chapter 10

He was unable to sleep. He thought of his parents and other parents who abandoned their children. Who knows why they did not tie the knot? He lay on his bed, pondering over what may have been their own bitter reasons. His thoughts were totally chaotic, as though he were caught in a dust storm in the desert. Far away, he can see isolated green patches. The sinking sun has turned the dunes red. As the sun sets, there is nothing but darkness.

Sarah, too, was awake. She has yet to know the total outcome of the meeting. Daniel did not reveal the date of the farewell. She can be sure of freedom, free from the present uncertainty, and free from Seema Ma'am.

"Sarah, are you sleeping?" he asked.

"No, what about you? I am sure you want to say something if you feel it is okay; otherwise, don't worry," Sarah said.

It was nearly 1 a.m. They could both see the wall clock in the light of the night lamp.

"We are leaving soon. From here and from school," Daniel said.

She turned her body towards him and locked his body in the grip of her legs. Her breath was strong. It was as if she had gotten back her lost toy after the whole day's play.

"Sarah, I belong only to you," he affirmed.

"I know, and I have only you," she said.

She pushed his head into her bosom like a mother who takes care of her child when it is in deep sorrow. She was crying. It is true no one can take her child from her warm bosom—he rested, he is at peace—the calmness he felt when he went to the deepest bed of the sea after escaping from the undercurrents of the turbulent waves. Let me be there forever; may the night be long with them lost in the darkness.

The next morning, Daniel slept in late. Sarah watched him as he curled up like a baby.

"Look, open your eyes; it is 7 a.m. You do not want to go to school?" Sarah asked.

He felt as if it were a mother asking her child.

"I must go because there are no more secrets; all the school now knows that we are leaving," Daniel explained.

"Your breakfast is almost ready. Your tiffin box is yet to be packed."

"Yes, Sarah, thanks. I will be ready soon. Finally, your prayers are heard in heaven and on earth. Ma'am is happy that you and I are headed for a better future. We are teachers; only the end result is important. All through the year, some students are not regular in their studies, but they still do well in exams. That is the teacher's attitude," Daniel said philosophically.

"Are you happy, or do you still have second thoughts?" Sarah asked.

"No, dear, she said to me there are hardly six months left for her retirement; this is the best she can do for us," he said.

"She is fond of you and loves you. Only a mother can do what she did. Maybe she is your lost mother. How can we know?" Sarah wondered.

Daniel did not answer. All he said was, "I hope you are happy now."

She was silent and went to his side, where he was sitting on the bed with his legs resting on the floor. She took his head in both hands, patted him on the shoulder, and kissed him on his forehead and cheeks. That was her answer. He felt she was at peace.

The anticipated farewell would be a great event, and, of course, he had no choice in the matter. Not because he hates anyone—no enemies, no friends—but because that is the way he lived and spent the time on the school campus. As usual, he heard the same footsteps come in, and once he had waited with excitement for their coming with her note, compounded with anxiety, but today he was relaxed.

"Sir, Ma'am wants to see you immediately," the peon came in with the request.

"Anything urgent?"

"No idea Sir. Please do come," he said.

Daniel casually walked into the corridor. He could not think of any situation that called for this urgency. There must be some delay in the departure date. As he walked into her cabin, she was her usual graceful and happy self, wearing her favourite pink sari of the season. From the expression on her face, he felt she wanted to discuss something very important.

"Good morning, Daniel. Please take a seat."

"Thanks, Ma'am."

"How is Sarah? And how are you?"

"Both are fine; everything is OK."

"Good. This is all I wish for you. I called you in to know what was on your mind about the staff and students wanting to give you and Sarah a farewell. They have informed me that they would love to give you a farewell and a gift, and so they wanted to know your choice," Seema asked.

"I had no choice then or now. If you can avoid it, I will be very happy. The reason behind it is that I do not want to carry the message that I left the school in the middle of the curriculum, which may break my heart, so please let me cherish my memory and continue in my endeavours." Daniel finished his reply in one breath.

She removed her reading glasses and rubbed her eyelids and forehead for a while.

"I respect your feelings and sentiments. I spent fifteen years of my thirty-five-year career at this institution, which is about to come to an end. Sometimes we have to compromise on our own to show respect for the feelings of others. There is nothing wrong with that. Our moral values and dedication will remain in everyone's memory, and our integrity will forever be remembered. The great respect we receive will have an everlasting impact on our lives. So don't be rigid, and please bring Sarah along with you next Saturday. I will be personally calling her. I am taking this liberty and am sure you will not let me down," Seema said.

"Never, not in this birth," Daniel replied.

"Thank you. The farewell programme is fixed for Saturday at 3.30 p.m.," she said.

"Thanks ma'am. May I take your leave? Thank you once again." He bowed his head out of respect before he took leave.

Seemaji, without raising her head, her specs in hand, was rubbing her forehead, and in a very low voice, she said, "Bye, Daniel; God bless you and Sarah."

"Bye Ma'am." He left the room, softly shutting the door behind him.

Chapter 11

Mrs. Mary Antony sat in her high-back chair, mentally going over the events of the day, as she did every day before leaving for home. Today's highlight was the new art teacher who had joined the faculty. Ashok M. Daniel, a strapping young man, had been recommended by her good friend Seema Chopra from Delhi. In fact, he worked at the Delhi International school. It was odd that Seemaji let go of her staff while she was still the principal. But Mary did not dwell on it. She was simply grateful that her school had a good art teacher.

She met Daniel for the first time today. He had not been asked to come for an interview because of Seemaji's confidence in his talent and abilities. He came across as someone calm and composed, in contrast to the new job applicants, who are usually a bundle of nerves when they first arrive. The unfamiliar surroundings and the flight from India did not appear to have bothered him in any way.

Mary tried to concentrate on the other events of the day, but somehow the young man was all she could think about. That morning, a current had run down her spine as she met his extended hand. It was a magical feeling, one she didn't have words to explain. Was it simply because the arts teacher had studied in Lucknow? She had so desperately attempted, but failed, to erase from her memory the city of Nawabs and its gift to her. Or was it because he reminded her of what should have been her most cherished possession that circumstances took away from her?

He would be all grown up today. Would he not be like Daniel today? They should be around the same age.

She was a strong woman. A woman known for her tenacity, determination, values, and unwavering work ethics. But today, as she sat slumped in her chair, she looked like someone who had lost the war.

It was the year 1984. A tumultuous year for the country and an equally tumultuous year for Mary. While the country witnessed Prime Minister Indira Gandhi's assassination, which was followed by violent anti-Sikh riots, young Mary was left scarred for life when she was forced to give up her newborn baby. While most wounds heal with time, this one would never heal.

A graduate nurse Mary Jacob, had just completed two years as a staff nurse at the Christian Mission Hospital in the north Indian city of Lucknow. A BSc nursing graduate from her hometown in Kerala, Mary was a Syrian Christian by faith. She was known for her rather dutiful disposition. It was during her night shift in the month of October that she met ACP Meher Rai.

A Tamil Nadu cadre Indian Police Service officer, ACP Rai, was admitted following a fracture to his calf bone of the right leg due to a bike accident. Sister Shiny, Mary's friend and colleague, was told that Rai was arrogant and easily irritable. And as she was not comfortable dealing with the injured officer, she requested that Mary take over her night duties.

When fate decides, there is little that men can do. She accepted Shiny's request and took on the night duties. They say opposites attract. If that is true, then that was it. Mary and Meher had little in common, yet very soon they became intimate friends. She came from a middle-class family in the deep South. He was from an affluent and deeply entrenched patriarchal setup in the northern state of Rajasthan. Culturally, there was a wide divide, and yet the two had never felt the difference.

He was on deputation to Lucknow, and he was to return to Madras after his deputation tenure ended. Their relationship was unconditional and uncommitted. Neither made any demands on the other. What was that instinct that made her meet him again and again during those three months he was in Lucknow? Was this love? Or was it that she too wanted to experience what she had only heard about from her friends and colleagues? Was it just a biological need that prompted her to give her all to a man who had not made any commitments? Or was it the fallacies of youth that made you love with such gay abandon and then part without remorse or regret?

She'd be lying if she said she had no remorse or regret. Perhaps that was the case on his end. She will never know. She tried to put herself in his shoes, but she couldn't come up with an appropriate response. Whatever his reasons, she let it be. Sitting at her office table, 30 years later, she still clearly remembers every word he said that last evening.

"I will remember you and cherish your memory till my last day. I will not be calling you again, as my profession demands certain discipline and work ethics to either continue or quit. That is the only choice. Knowing all this, I entered into an affair that I cannot justify. May I confess that after our first meeting, there was no control left in me? How do I define my feelings? Please, Mary, at least say one word at this moment. Do you expect anything from me?" Meher asked.

She just smiled and bit her lower lip, the tears falling from her eyes. He wiped her eyes with both thumbs and kissed her on both cheeks and her forehead. She stood there like a statue.

"Will we meet again?" he asked.

"I don't know," Mary said.

There was no parting kiss or hug. She stood there like a rock, unable to move or react. Even today, she could still feel the strength of his thumbs on her cheeks, as if they had left a permanent mark. The sound of his brown leather shoes was like a horse's canter as he walked away. She could hear the police jeep moving away and disappearing forever.

How did everything happen so fast? How the time had passed! A beautiful relationship started like a wildfire and ended abruptly without leaving a trail. Not once, from either his or her side, have they demanded or expressed a desire to marry and live together.

Mary had no idea that she would have to pay a high price for her fleeting happiness. She realized later that departure would leave such a void in her life. Despite the fact that they only met once a week, she began to feel lonely.

Many of her high school and college classmates would talk about their flirting and romance. She, too, dreamt of falling in love one day. What kind of experience would that be? But she never fell in love with anyone at her high school or college. Celine, her eldest sister, even married a man she was secretly dating. Her husband, like Mary's parents, worked as teachers. For the rest of the world, it was an arranged marriage, but Celine had known her prospective groom before the wedding. He was a frequent visitor to their neighbourhood, and he came to meet Celine under the guise of meeting his relatives.

What was most important to Mary, however, was finishing her nursing course. Her parents had never asked her to do anything except complete her studies successfully. They were both middle school teachers, no other significant income apart from their profession, living a normal life. While nursing was regarded as a noble profession, her mom and dad, like most parents of girls of marriageable age, hoped it would aid in the search for a well-established groom settled abroad.

She wished in her heart that some guy would also propose to her. She also wanted to fall under the spell of romance. Maybe it was her dark complexion and tall, athletic build that turned off young men.

So it came as an utter surprise when, on the second night of her duty, while she was administering the medicines, Meher Rai asked, "Why did you choose nursing as a career?"

Mary was taken aback. He had never spoken to her. Quickly gathering her wits about her, she asked, "Why? Do you think I am not good at nursing?"

"No, sister, I meant with your personality and looks, you should have been in the police or civil service."

"Police or civil service?" "No one has said this to me before," she replied with a smile.

The IPS officer's comment had totally floored her. It was a huge compliment for her. He had seen something special in her. She had the personality to be a police officer!

She reminded herself that she had to check with her colleagues to see if this was his pick-up line. If he was also complimenting the other nurses as well. If he was a flirt and a master at flattery,

Despite her reservations, Mary was looking for reasons to spend more time with him, unknown to herself. She began making arrangements for when and how she could be nearby in pretext to help him without drawing attention to herself.

"Am I dreaming?" she would ask herself many times. A handsome man, well-mannered and well-established—an IPS officer no less—was paying her attention. In her last two years of service at the hospital, she had attended to many patients, both men and women. But hardly did anyone bother having a conversation beyond thanking her for her sincerity and kindness. Meher Rai was different.

Mary started keeping a diary soon after Meher was admitted. Previously, the diary only had phone numbers and details of the birthdays of her friends. Now, she scrupulously started writing about every little incident regarding Meher. His interest made her look at herself in a new light. When an unknown person appreciates or recognises an individual, it is their personality that is being appreciated. In her case, Meher Rai had seen her potential in her personality.

She can only recall being a high school basketball player and an athlete in race events. Her instructor in physical education once told her, "Mary, walk straight; you have a nice figure; otherwise, your neck will grow a hump. Straighten up." She never let him down.

Why had she chosen nursing? She did not have an answer. She questioned herself. But it was the chosen profession for most of her classmates as well. It was her profession that assured her a secure job. Did she think she had any other potential? Not really.

It was also the first time a man other than her father showed an interest in her. During their conversations at night, when all the other patients were sleeping, Mary and Meher would have their little chats. Meher, for his part, wanted to know more about Mary, her background and family, and what she did in her spare time.

Mary was counting down the days until he was released from the hospital while he was progressively recuperating. When he would be sent to physiotherapy after his plaster was removed, she would stare at his vacant bed and wait for him to return to the ward. Hospitals' principal role is to cure or help patients recover and to discharge them as quickly as possible. The irony was that Mary's heart wished for him to spend more days in the ward.

In Mary's opinion, his eyes and language have always displayed an incredible eagerness. He might be timid. How is it possible for a cop to be timid? They deal with thugs, criminals, and innocent victims while constantly interacting with the public like she does. The distinction is that he dressed in khaki can be rough and commanding, while she in her nursing whites has to be soft and tender as a healer. The two colours are incredibly unlike each other.

However, they too are in a pitiful state when they arrive at the hospital for treatment, and they deserve attention. Despite their apparent roughness and hardness, they behave much more civilly outside of the police station. There, large sticks and muscular police officers display their strength. But they are so afraid of the little scissors and needles in the hospital. She repeatedly noticed this aspect of human behaviour during her nursing profession. The human mind is a baffling thing. Mary has observed how the human psyche changes when a person is ill and bedridden; they feel lost forever and helpless. Here, too, she felt the same way. She felt that a well-built, handsome, qualified, and strong man at his prime age with a minor accident was seeking nearness, affection, and love.

Mary knew she had to handle this relationship with Meher with utmost care. She learned from fellow nurses that relationships with patients could turn very sour. What she felt for him was way beyond the call of duty. She had to make sure other patients did not feel neglected or that was giving undue attention to one particular patient. That would tarnish her records, and yet she was unable to help.

As her duty was at night, she hardly knew who would come to see him during the day. She remembered hearing Shiny mention that he had visitors one after another, either siblings or office staff.

"Mary, yesterday, my mama was here for a long time. I sincerely missed you and wanted to introduce you to her. Sorry, I meant to introduce my mother to you, but you are always on night duty. Moreover, she cannot come alone and only comes with my staff."

Meher said this to her as if he knew in her mind that she wanted to meet his relatives.

"Thanks, Mr. Meher that is okay. Yes, I was even thinking I had not seen any of your relatives. What about your dad and siblings?" Mary replied in her usual tone without showing any eagerness.

"Sorry, Mary, my father died in an accident; he was a bureaucrat in the IAS. I am the only son, and I have one sister who is a professor in Jaipur. I hail from Rajasthan and opted for the Tamil Nadu cadre IPS, but my father was a Kerala cadre IAS, so I studied quite a lot of Malayalam words. Since my father's death, my mother lives in Jaipur, Rajsthan." Meher had explained.

He knows Malayalam? Goodness! Her mind tried to quickly rifle down old conversations from the past 10 days with Shiny or any of the other Malayalee co-workers to remember if she had said anything untoward during duty changes. While they must uphold professional ethics, the sisters have occasionally made jokes and comments about patients that aren't meant to be hurtful or to upset any particular patient.

Still, flustered by the revelation about his knowing Malaylam, she thanked him and tried to move away to the other patients. But Meher was keen to continue the conversation.

"Excuse me, Mary, you never told me anything about your family."

Without giving it much thought or simply because she was a little disconcerted, she retorted: "In our ward, there are fifty patients; all of them have various ailments and are very demanding. Both the hospital and the patient are unaware of how one nurse meets their expectations, and if we began to recount personal details or listen to all the patients, you can well picture what would happen then." His face went red as if he had uttered something inappropriate.

She immediately understood her mistake. She had ticked him off by comparing him to all the other patients. Now she felt guilty.

"Mary, I'm sorry," he quickly apologised and added, "If my memory serves me right, I have never been admitted to the hospital before. I was feeling very lonely, not having found anyone to communicate with. Sorry again,"

His statement left her feeling guiltier. "Do not say sorry. We are all human."

She could have simply said, "Sorry, Mr. Meher, I am busy; maybe some other time." He was making all the efforts to be friendly, and she failed him. 'What type of person are you, Mary?' She scolded herself.

Her reasoning told her that she was exaggerating his interest in her, but her heart refused to believe it. His comments, such as how he wanted her to meet his mother when she visited him in the hospital, reinforced her belief that their feelings were mutual. This was her first taste of romance, and before long, she was head over heels in love with Meher. Every moment of her spare time she wanted to spend with him. Mary saw love and affection in his eyes and touch, despite the fact that he had never once committed to keeping in touch with her after he left. Therefore, it was only natural that after he was discharged, they started meeting outside the hospital. She was happy to be with him in every sense of the word.

It had been two months since he had left her standing at her door when she realised that her first romance had not left her empty-handed; she was carrying the gift of his love. For the first few days, she did not know how to react. When the enormity of the situation sank in, she got in touch with her mother. Being devout Christians, her parents were against her aborting the baby.

So, on one cold winter morning in December, exactly six days after her little angel was born, a sobbing Mary had to make the harshest decision of her life. She decided to say goodbye to her child. Aided by her mother, she approached the Missionaries of Charity in Delhi and left her baby in their care.

She was barely 23. She decided to take life by the horns. In consultation with her parents, she decided to go overseas as soon as her bond period was over at Mission Hospital in Lucknow.

It was not long before Mary was headed for a job in a Dubai hospital. Like a lot of Keralites who went to the Gulf countries in the 1990s, Mary too decided to fly off to Dubai. One of the best offers that came Mary's way was to be a staff nurse in a hospital run by Abdul Al Rashid, one of the most prominent families in the Emirates. In a span of 25 years, she is now heading the Abdul Al Rashid family's trust-run school, the Dubai International School.

Her diligence, abilities, and, most importantly, integrity saw her rise through the ranks very quickly. Within a few years, she was heading the nursing department as senior matron. Impressed with her personality and work ethics, the Al Rashid's offered her the position of mentor and family nurse for their children. A position most of her well-wishers felt would not be conducive. It would mean an end to her nursing career in hospitals if she became the home nurse for a family. Aside from that, her job would be at the mercy of her employer's whims and fancies, and if she were fired, she would be unable to find work in any hospital in the

Gulf. Mary, however, decided to take a calculated risk and take on the assignment.

Her decision to quit the hospital and become a house nurse was, however, based solely on her intuition and her faith in a higher power, although initially she was reluctant to take it up. It proved to be a turning point in her career. Everything could have gone awry. But as they say, fortune favours the bold. So it was in Mary's case. Her bond with the Sheikh's family became so strong that they came to regard her as one of their most valued members.

Mary had impressed Sheikha Nabeesa when she was assigned to care for her in the hospital at the birth of her first child. During the births of her next two children, the Sheikha insisted on Mary being delegated to care for her. And when her third child arrived, the Princess was certain that no one was more suitable than Mary to be entrusted with the care of her little ones.

Soon after the Sheikha went home with her infant, Mary was summoned for an interview at the Palace. The Sheikh and his wife requested that she resign from her position as senior matron in their hospital and instead become a home nurse and caretaker solely for their own children. That was five years ago.

As the years passed and children were old enough to enter kindergarten, she was told that Her Highness wanted to share with her about a new project.

"I am aware of your past in the medical field, particularly as a committed nurse, Mrs. Mary. I'm going to make you an offer right now, so you may consider it and respond to us after speaking with your husband, Mr. Anthony. Although we are the founders of numerous institutions, the administration of our organisation has never dabbled in education. However, we have now decided to start our own school and believe that you should take charge of it and serve as its principal."

For a moment, she was caught off guard. Did she really hear what she was told? Despite her excitement, she realised it would be a formidable task and a new challenge for her. She pondered whether she should act or not. Although she was aware of her inadequacies, but had no option. She must answer 'yes'; otherwise, she will have to keep serving as 'a home nurse and caretaker'. She has one more opportunity to open the door to a vast new sky.

"Yes, Ma'am, thank you so much for your belief in my abilities, but I doubt that I will be able to live up to your expectations in terms of performance and managing an institution," she concluded in one breath.

"Mary, individuals who don't have the ambition to grow and rise to bigger heights express doubts. Your doubts are very genuine, and you know my husband has many businesses, from hospitals and hospitality to construction, and we have ventured into more than twenty-four different companies. But he is not an engineer, a doctor, or someone with a background in hotel management. What you need are the skills to manage people. Ever since you joined our family, I have never found any difficulty in your managing the house and our children. Now that they are growing, I find you have much more time to devote to helping my husband," the Sheikha said.

"To find the correct person for the right job and place them in the right place is the task, so the institution can turn into a healthy, prosperous one. We find you have the potential, and we believe you can perform and establish this new school. Select the right people for the right job, place them in the appropriate position so that their egos, efficiency, and capability can be matched, and there they will become productive and efficient. You are a good listener; therein lies your success," she further added, trying to convince Mary.

She quietly listened to the wise counsel like an obedient worker. The Sheikha had praised Mary and kindly thanked her on numerous occasions. She was undoubtedly in a fairyland, something she had never dreamed of. She wanted to pinch herself to see if she was dreaming. Become the administrative head, lead the institution, and be a Trustee! One part of her was ecstatic, but the other tried to find a way to fight the change. She cherished the illustrious Sheikh's Palace and their lovely children as if they were her own. "Oh no! How will I balance the Palace and the institution if I embark on a new endeavour? I have loved and treasured them, and I never want to leave them ".

She went home and broke the news to Tony, her husband. Anthony Verkey, her husband, whom she lovingly called Tony at home, was a compassionate man. He never interfered in the running of their household. Their daily life was well defined. There was never a dearth of anything. There were no arguments or false ego trips. It was a blissful married life.

"Mary, they have confidence in you. Is there any place for scepticism? You need to say only one thing at the meeting tomorrow: 'I will do my best to live up to your expectations.'" Anthony advised.

During her meeting with the Sheikha, she mentioned that in the initial stage, the plan was to start from play school, kindergarten, and then go up to the eighth standard. "There should be a name that carries the theme of the school," Mrs. Nabeesa Sheikh mentioned at their meeting.

The Abdul Al Rashid's business empire had a very large team of people in every sector of work, and they had their own design team for advertising and branding their companies. Still, Mary knew she must be prepared to say something. In the Middle East, everything started with 'Al' but she didn't have any clue as to what name to give their school. She was very excited when she went to bed. But she soon fell asleep.

It was also not at all a restless night's sleep. Today, at the age of 51, she can look back with satisfaction. The "Matron" has successfully carried out her daily duties over the past 28 years. Her white uniform, complete with cap and overcoat, and confident smile had become her signature style. Everyone adored and admired her, from the medical staff to the patients, both within and outside the hospital. She held an uncontested position both in the hospital and at the Palace.

She could have written many stories and episodes if she had kept a daily diary for the last 28 years, but she had not been consistent and had never done it as a habit unless it was a very important event. Everyone may have similar stories in their profession, but there may be exceptions where they have had greater or lesser success.

Her circumstances and background from primary education to college had only one goal: to become a noble nurse, following in the path of 'Angel Nightingale' and living up to the expectations of her parents and professors. Probably now she can say, "YES!—I did it!'

From today on, it will be a new beginning in her life. Will she be able to justify the expectations they have of her? Her heart said, "Leave it to destiny. God has opened this door for me; He will guide me." She took a deep breath and repeated, I trust unto Thee". She woke up in good spirits and, with a fresh mind, began planning the start of a new phase of her life.

When she walked into the palace, the house attendant met her at the door and asked her to meet her employer, Sheikh Al Rashid. More than her, it appeared they were eagerly waiting to meet her.

"Good morning, Ma'am and your Highness," Mary wished them with a bowed head.

"Well, Mary, we believe you have given thought to what we discussed and proposed. Our children will be the first students at the school, along with yours," Sheikha said with a smile.

She spoke with such confidence, as if she knew her mind.

"Yes, your Highness," Mary endorsed.

The Sheikh explained that for the present year, the school will start with the pre-schoolers, and every year it will progress to the fifth grade. The immediate requirement for the school would be 15 teachers, including a principal. Mary would have to go to India for the recruitment of the teaching faculty. He emphasised that if the recruitment process is undertaken immediately, the prospective candidates will have sufficient time to give their notice period to leave their institution, and it will not adversely affect the students' academic year either.

"We will constitute a board for the management of the school, and Her Highness Sheikha Nabeesa will be the Chairperson. Mrs. Mary, you will be the President and Administrative Head. Now make up your mind and make preparations to go to India within fifteen days. All arrangements will be made accordingly. "We may not specify our preference for the candidates, but please keep in mind that those who teach in Christian schools and are Convent educated will be given preference," Sheikh said.

"Thank you, Your Highness, Ma'am." She bowed and left to begin her daily routine of taking care of the Palace and the children.

Though it was against her normal practice, today she made an exception and immediately sent a message to her husband. Normally, personal calls were not sent or received during office hours as a matter of ethics and discipline for her. She has ample leisure time for her family and personal life. Things were moving so fast that she sat down for a breather. Her mind was running faster than the speed of light. Just as she told herself to calm down, she remembered Meher Rai saying,

"Mary, this is your call; you are born to do much more and to reach bigger heights."

She felt as though she had just spoken to him. He had stormed into her life, leaving devastation in his wake. She had thought of calling him many times to tell him, 'I am pregnant,' soon after the pregnancy was confirmed. What had stopped her? Was it because she knew it was a no-strings-attached relationship? An IPS police officer in the very prime of his life and a young girl barely in her 21. Would he have rushed to her side if she had called him and announced, "I am pregnant"? What if he had taken her call as a threat? And worse still, if he had said, "You are in the medical profession; have an abortion." For the first four months of her pregnancy, she kept it a secret. On her tall, athletic body, it was not easy for someone to notice that she was pregnant.

Many cities were rebuilt after the tsunami. Mary, too, had built her life inch by inch, brick by brick. She was never going to make the same mistake of loving someone only for the sake of love. There was no time left for day-dreaming or post-mortems. Here, she had elevated herself to a position she had neither dreamed of nor demanded. But all her life, she never forgot his words, which had provided her with the impetus to scale higher heights.

She was well aware that her home was her only refuge. She had never kept a secret from her mother about her life. If she had told her mother about the police officer's hospitalisation and their intimacy, the story might have turned out differently. She usually called her mother on weekends to tell her about anything and everything. Why she kept the affair to herself is still a mystery to her. Perhaps she had no idea when she met him that it would lead to such a deep and intimate relationship culminating in motherhood, or perhaps she was afraid her mother would not approve.

There were no more misgivings. She has a dependable husband who understands and believes in her, and she is blessed to be the mother of twins, Aryan and Ananya. Her entire universe was encompassed in a single line: a loving, caring family. Her spouse and she both live in complete faith and understanding, and nothing else in life matters anymore.

Chapter 12

Daniel struggled to spread the large, rolled-up canvas. It had long been his dream since he left India to work on a bigger canvas. Thanks to Mary Ma, he has been given this huge space to work. He still remembered the limited space that he shared with three of his friends in Delhi's Sangam Vihar. The studio was very small and cramped with stacks of completed paintings, fresh canvases, paints, brushes, and other art materials. And one of the fondest memories was of the kettle that Surya had bought with his first income. It was a real saviour. Every time they needed an energy boost, they would put on the kettle to make themselves some green tea.

As an art teacher, neither the school nor the environment were ever suitable or conducive to larger-scale canvas experiments. Not only that, he never wanted to take unfair advantage of the school or set a bad example for his peers. Other teachers should not believe that being close to Seema Ma'am entitles him to special treatment. It's also not a good idea to stay late and use school for personal purposes. And when he went to his studio, Seemaji's work always took precedence.

And he would only do commercial assignments once in a while to cover his and Sarah's expenses. Life was going well, with no problems, but his subconscious mind was always asking one question. Is this all there is to life? Brother Vincent and other professors, his mentors, had high expectations of him. He recalls the quote vividly: "Many internationally renowned artists from Europe went by the name Daniel. You, too, will someday make us proud." During his almost six-year stay in Delhi, he visited a number of art galleries and met a number of artists. He could only participate in two or three group shows; he was never able to hold a solo show. For the favour and assistance he received from Seemaji, he was forced to sacrifice his life and his identity as an artist.

Is it out of anybody's compulsion? It was his choice, he could not blame anyone. Besides, Sarah was overjoyed with her financial security, which seemed to be the only goal for most married women's survival, from what Daniel could tell. At the end of the day, when he looks back today, he realises that whatever happened was for the best. He had landed a job within a short period of time after reaching Delhi. He had a place to stay and worked in the studio space shared with Surya. And Sarah is right too when she shows her gratitude for the blessings and prosperity showered on them. Yes, indeed, they were lucky. Thanks to Seemaji, he had managed to buy the house as well, so that Sarah too could come to Delhi.

The kind gesture of Surya introducing him to Seemaji was the turning point. After only three months of his arrival in the national capital, he had a chance encounter at the Delhi Centre of Art that forever changed his life. Meeting Seema Ma'am opened the doors of fortune for him. Being given a chance as a novice was pure fate. Without thinking twice, Surya suggested and presented him to her.

Daniel was in the exhibition hall when Seema Chopra asked if Surya would like to join her school as a substitute art teacher. But he declined, citing his commercial assignments and upcoming solo show.

"But I have a friend two years my junior in college who is very much here. If you ask him, you should not feel that I am recommending him. Just talk to him. If he is up to your expectations, then only you may like to give him a try." Surya had suggested.

"Your junior from Lucknow College of Art? Then I don't need any further scrutiny. If he is nearby, please call him to ask if he can come to school tomorrow," Seemaji replied in a very low tone.

Daniel was checking out artist Vijender Sharma's intricate work, full of colours, when Surya came and patted him on the back.

"Come, meet Mrs. Seema Chopra. She's Principal of Delhi International School. She is looking for an art teacher, as the teacher left before the curriculum on health grounds. Come and speak to her." Daniel followed Surya.

She was sitting opposite the curator's table when Surya introduced Daniel.

"Mr. Daniel, meet me at 11.30 a.m. in my school," she said, handing him her visiting card.

After she left, Surya told Daniel about Seema Chopra's reach and capabilities and what working with her could mean for his future.

"Daniel, you met a very influential lady, Principal of a renowned school. Once she likes you, rest assured, your career is made. For the time being, it is a leave vacancy, but it is likely to be continued. I will tell you the location, take an auto-rickshaw and go," Surya said with authority.

In later days, when he and Seemaji became good friends, she confided that his appearance was totally deceptive. She said that when she first saw him, she was suspicious and wondered if he could really be an art teacher. By no means did he look like an art teacher or match the stereo typed perceptions of an artist—he did not have a slouch or a stained shoulder bag, and he was not dramatically serious. Instead, he was sporting ironed pants and a shirt and polished shoes, had the walk and physique of a sportsman, and wore a natural smile. Why did this young man opt to do art? As a young 23-year-old, he should have been a model or actor. And added with mock drama, you certainly are in the wrong profession young man! you could well be a model or actor. He smiled to himself as he went about getting his canvas ready. At a later time, when they were alone at her place, he confided in her about his childhood. Seema had been very understanding and sympathetic. And they had developed an inexplicable bond that went beyond accepted definitions.

Almost five years have passed since he joined the school in Dubai. How fast has time flown? Dubai was an entirely unique experience. He started out as an art instructor before rising to the position of head and mentor at the faculty of art, which gave him the opportunity to arrange exhibitions and facilitate additional exposure outside the classroom for the students.

Dubai's culture is distinct from Delhi's. There, gossiping is a fervent habit, and even the peons and sweepers are aware of everything that goes on in the school administration, including salary, personal affairs, who loves whom, and who is friends with whom. In contrast to Delhi, he does not speak when parents or students enquire about scholastic activities here because he lacks the authority to do so. He is also aware that any slip of the tongue could result in unintended complications.

Although he doesn't feel insecure in this environment, he isn't afraid to confess that there are some constraints on freedom here. For example, there isn't any unwelcome conversation, gossip, or breaking news in the cafeteria. The way of life is really straightforward: sign the register, note and comment on all of your daily tasks, then go about your business as usual. Simply meet or contact the required person through the intercom if there is any need. The administration will act quickly to address any needs and provide assistance. All suggestions and requirements are recorded in the minutes of the weekly review meetings. Remedial measures are taken in a time-bound manner.

The Dubai International School (DIS) was established in 1990. In the few years since its inception, the school, headed by Mrs. Mary Anthony, has made great strides and is now one of the most sought-after schools in the Emirati city. This institution is one of the many ventures that SBS Trust holds in the city. His Highness of SBS of Dubai and his wife are the owners of the school. The AL Saqr International School was established in 1990. Mrs. Mary Anthony is directly in charge and has sole responsibility beyond that as the administrator. In her career as principal and trusted member of the Trust, Ms. Mary has always been given full liberty to explore new avenues that work for the betterment of the institution. Her educational background as a nurse was never a barrier to holding the trust of the Al Rashid family, and the Sheikh's persuasion prompted her to accept and take responsibility for running the school without any difficulties.

Her Highness The Sheikha never meets or interacts with any staff. Daniel had the opportunity to see Her Highness once at their school's annual function. Till now, they had only up to V grade, and at that function, she announced the school was going to be upgraded to X grade within four years, and you all are going to be passed out after X grade from this institution. The whole audience stood up, clapped, and cheered her. The emotional parents couldn't stop the clapping until Mrs. Mary announced that they should be seated.

For Daniel, the day is dawning to fulfil last night's aspirations and make up for the lost years to achieve artistic success in Delhi. Though he made money and material wealth, his sole regret is that he was unable to pursue his style of work. He had to create the artwork required for Seemaji and the gallery's on-demand sales. He will, though, always be grateful to Seemaji for suggesting his name to Mary Anthony and for the opportunity she gave him.

His new job has left him with plenty of time to work beyond school hours and complete his goals. He was quite careful and sought the administration's approval before working on the school premises. When he asked for permission, Mary Ma'am was quite kind and supportive. "You can use all the resources and space you need. The school will be so proud. Young man, it is the prestige of the school that inspires the students to experiment and comprehend art not only as a hobby but also as having the potential to bring commercial value in the future."

She once enquired about his after-school activities in Delhi and the location of his studio, where he stored his artwork.

He was speechless and unsure of how she would respond to an honest response. She is the head of the school administration, and for reasons he could not fully explain, he was unable to respond.

"Ma…" Instead of Madam, Daniel stumbled, and she didn't even show any signs of irritation or unhappiness. She smiled innocently, as if a mother were asking her child a question and realising he was trying to tell a lie.

"Ma'am, for beginners like us, it is costly to rent a private studio in its Delhi. There, my buddies and I used to share a small space—say 200 square feet—where we could only manage medium-sized paintings." He was perspiring.

He wondered whether Seemaji had ever disclosed to her that he was the behind-the-scenes boy for her projects. He had to save the day. It appeared that Mary Ma'am is a psychologist, just like Seemaji. She seemed to comprehend his mental state, he thought. She enquired amiably, "Would you like to have a cup of tea?"

He remained silent, but she called the peon and ordered tea.

Daniel remarked, "That was a time of extreme struggle, and we tried everything for our survival and to meet our financial issues."

"There's nothing wrong with it, so that's great. Hard work pays off in the end, so it's a good indicator," she remarked.

"Indeed, Ma'am. Frankly, I liked working on commerical projects," a dejected Daniel added. The peon came in with tea, and Daniel's hand was not steady while picking up the tea cup. His mind was questioning his integrity, as if he had overexpressed himself or hidden some truth.

"Have tea; nothing serious; I just asked. Go ahead. If there's anything you need—space or material—you can use the annexe building, which has just been finished and has empty space available for future expansion of our school. You can use any classroom that suits you."

"Thanks, Ma'am, I am very grateful for your kindness, which I could never dream of. If I could have this…" He couldn't complete the sentence.

Again, she called the peon and told him to help Daniel and give him a classroom in the annexe building. She instructed the office head to give him all the assistance and give him one key so that he could work and use the space at any time.

"Thank you so much." He was so excited, he just wanted to share the happy news with Sarah. He thought, "Let me wait to get out of here." After he finished the tea, he was reluctant to ask her permission to leave and waited until she finished her tea, as he remembered the table manners he was taught at the boarding school. She continued the conversation, asking,

"How are you enjoying the school ambience and working environment? If there's anything more you need, feel at liberty to tell me directly."

Then, as he got up to leave, she asked, "Do you have any reservations if we bring our children to where you work? You both did a wonderful job with Aryan and Ananya's birthdays. Everyone liked the theme of the animal kingdom, which all the children enjoyed. Our children became your fans, and Anthony Sir liked Sarah's Kerala cuisine."

"Thanks, Sarah also likes their company. You can bring them at any time. Some artists are very particular. They don't want visitors in their working studio; I don't know why. But I do love to interact and chat with students."

After finishing the tea, she got to her feet and offered her hand. He felt as though lightning had touched his heart and flowed through his veins as his palm brushed her soft palms. He is unable to adequately describe a touch that is both mesmerising and sincere.

'This hand will be painted. It has a spiritual quality about it.' He told himself.

"Bye Daniel, take care, and give my regards to Sarah."

He stood for a moment. "Sure, Ma, I will. Thanks again."

She had not shown any surprise when he addressed her as Ma; probably she felt it was not done intentionally.

When he came out of the Admin Room, he wanted to run and raise his hand to the sky and say, "My prayers are heard." Who is this angel? He is so excited that he murmurs, "Sarah, I love you."

He wanted to rush to the classroom to tell the students and scream to the whole world, but he held himself back. As tears of joy ran down his face, he cried, "These wings of mine are now unclipped and untied. All irregular contours will appear to be smooth mountain terrain above the sea as I soar to the highest point in the boundless sky."

He took out his mobile phone to call Sarah but immediately realised it was school time and it was not allowed to use phones on campus. The beats of his heart were so fast that only Sarah could calm him down. He had another two hours before he could reach home. He had to keep his excitement under control. For an artist, more than anything, a big space to hold bigger canvases and colours is their world. Once the bird is able to leave the nest, the sky is the limit. He, too, felt the same way.

To whom all should he say thanks? To all his mentors, Seemaji, Brother Vincent, Surya, and friends, and of course Sarah, because of their help, he has come to this stage.

He remembered noting in his diary, "The unknown mother who did not kill her child, how much pain she must have gone through to keep him alive in her womb. For me, it is just that I was born out of wedlock, but who is that brave woman who, at her virginal age, could bear a child? Maybe I was born out of rape. Oh no, then there would have been hatred, and she would have had the abortion. I might have been born out of immense love, with my unknown father leaving without a trace. Can it be certain that there was a certain amount of hatred between them? Certainly not. She wanted her child to be born, a courageous woman, divine in heart, who could stand all the odds and troubles."

He looked up at the sky and murmured, "Thank you, Ma, blessed is your womb." He had a good memory of the MC Sisters. They all looked alike in their pure white saris with blue borders. He also faintly remembers an old lady who was very fragile, and whenever she came, there was feasting and the distribution of gifts and sweets to all the children. Thank you, angels; like many others, he too could see the light for years to come.

He faintly remembered that all the children there were toddlers and pre-schoolers. Many times, they had some very fair-skinned visitors. Later, he learned they were mostly Europeans. They came bearing lots of gifts and hung around with the children. Some stayed for a few months.

When they left, one of the kids would disappear with them. Mostly, it would be a girl.

As he turned 10, Daniel and four other boys bid goodbye to the MC Sisters. They were sent off to the Orphanage of the Gabriel Brothers. It was an exciting yet sad day, Daniel recalls. They were thrilled at the prospect of travelling in an open jeep, yet leaving the sisters and what they knew as home was daunting for them. The boys were nicknamed 'Pandavas' by the Gabriel Brothers.

The separation from the MC Sisters Ashram happened to coincide with one of the sisters' birthdays. Daniel distinctly remembered her because she addressed the children as God's children born with a special purpose to serve the world. Her words had left an indelible imprint on his young heart. She was a soft-spoken, frail woman, and her wrinkled face glowed in the candlelight when she cut the cake. Daniel realised she was none other than Saint Mother Teresa as he grew older. 'Thank you, Sisters.'

Discipline was the essence and the most used word on all occasions at the Gabriel Brothers. Everything was the same as with the MC Sisters, except that there were no soft hands to pat you. All were equals in the hostel—the same parental status, the same dormitory. Love was lost in a strict world.

When he reached the 6th standard, Daniel realised that merit was awarded not only by the marks scored but also by attitude and discipline, which were always considered and were the main criteria for promotions. As the boys grew taller and taller, there were strict orders that everyone participate in sports, athletics, creative art, and choir. Everyone had to be involved in everything and everywhere; participation was more important than competition.

From the fifth standard on, it was "talent hunting" time. Each brother had his own set of preferences, outlooks, and methods. Once the brothers grow fond of you, they become extremely possessive and train you in arts, music, athletics, theatre, and drama according to your aptitude. One of the brothers, Br. Vincent, was quite strict and almost never smiled. He only gave directives, never requests. He painted all the famous biblical figures because he was an enthusiastic painter. Throughout his early education in Italy, where he spent a lot of time, it was his hobby.

After school and on weekends, Daniel's responsibility was to dust the studio when Brother Vincent finished his work. He also cleaned the palette and brushes. He was thirteen. He was permitted to use pencils, charcoal, and crayons since he was too young to handle paint. He would invite two of his pals, but once they left, he roamed the studio alone.

Daniel, while working on his own canvas, recalled how Brother Vincent would call him and his friends before finishing the work to see the work he had done. Daniel hated the smell of turpentine, linseed oil, and kerosene. They all smell dirty. As usual, he would stand in one corner of the studio and watch how he brought life to the blank canvas. He was meticulous and very serious, never letting his attention wander. His discipline and diligence made it almost meditative. Young Daniel would stand by and watch as he prepared the spotless white canvas, applying the base coat over and over, then mixing some vibrant colours and making the strokes with a broad brush. Once, he caught Daniel standing there alone, watching his work. He asked him in a very loud and rough voice,

'Why are you hanging around? Why don't you go with your friends to play?'

"'I like colours."

"You mean, you like the colours but don't want to do the painting? That is funny."

"Yes, I like colours and painting. I can do the preparation of the canvas for you."

"So I will give you the canvas till you learn the basics of how to prepare the canvas. It is important to do this before you become an artist or painter. Okay?' Suddenly, his voice was gentle.

That was the defining moment in Daniel's life. After that, it became his daily routine. As a teacher, Brother Vincent always encouraged Daniel to join him in the studio. He would inform him in advance so that Daniel would keep himself free to join him.

When his batch was promoted to the 12th standard, he cautioned Daniel and his classmates, 'This year, no art, no studio, no sports. Just concentrate on studying. It is a crucial year. Unless you score a good percentage in your respective class, you can never get admission into a professional college.'

Though he generally came across as tough, when it came to Daniel, he showed a much softer, more caring side. 'If you have any difficulty with any subject, you must let me know. Are you sure your ultimate choice is Arts college?' he asked Daniel, when the young boy had expressed his desire to become an artist. Daniel could even today, after so many years, feel the fatherly love hidden in his voice.

"Except for a few occasions, such as the day of the PTA meeting, I didn't miss the presence of my parents. I don't know where they are or what prompted them to leave me in the hands of the MC Sisters. It could have been that I was born out of wedlock or they could not afford to bring me up." That was a remote possibility, because hardly ever would parents leave a boy in an orphanage. Most of the orphans were girls because the parents thought it would be a burden to marry them off when they grew up. Hence, Daniel was sure he was a child conceived out of deep love between two individuals and may have been their accidental child.

'For me, life was so enchanting, and it hardly gave me time for any introspection.' But still, before the board examinations, he had asked Brother Vincent what to fill in the column for parents and guardians on his college admission forms.

'Why do you worry? If someone doesn't want to take you, why do you take the unnecessary botheration? Just fill in the word 'orphan' in the column, under guardian, and you can write Gabriel Brothers. Your religion is on record. On the slip your mother left, there was one sentence written: 'My child is Christian.' Brother Vincent had assured him.

Daniel had remained silent. Brother Vincent had been concerned, for he knew from Daniel's expression that the young boy felt let down.

"Sincerely, from the core of my heart, I believe if God blesses me, one day I will meet my mother, who gave me birth. She is an angel with all the odds thrown at her, but she had the courage to face the world. She should have had the abortion done in the first or second month of pregnancy. Why did she prolong it? She may have thought and been hoping against hope that he would marry her. The man must have been a coward and never wanted to face the social taboo of a child born out of wedlock. No parent will accept a woman who had an affair before marriage; they will label her a "loose woman'." But Daniel was very sure she was certainly a brave woman, ready to face the wrath of all consequences. So I am a much wanted child. That was always his conviction.

"I have always hoped that one day, when I become a grown-up man, my first mission will be to find out who my mother is." Daniel would time and again share with Sarah his childhood dream of finding his roots. But Sarah never encouraged him. "'Why do you bother? They have given us birth. They didn't kill us. The only difference is that I am a girl,'

"There is a possibility that they may be poor. Could it be a financial burden? It could be that I was born out of wedlock, the ultimate child of a deep courtship. It can or may not be." Sarah never bothered and had a 'don't care' attitude. She never wanted to carry the baggage of unwanted emotions and sentiments. She had a very different outlook on life.

That evening back home, he asked Sarah: "When many of our childhood friends were adopted and went abroad with European parents, all living in luxury, why no one came forward to adopt any one of us?"

"God heard my prayers."

"What prayers?"

"It is because of my earnest prayers that no one adopted us." "Do you remember how we met the very first time?"

Much to Daniel's chagrin, Sarah narrated in detail how once during choir practice he was made to stand behind her. Father placed all the girls in the front row, and you were positioned behind my back," Sarah narrated with much innocence.

"What?" Daniel asked in shock.

"Yes, Daniel, my dear, we were both almost the same age but in different classes. Until the choir practice was over, you were holding my right elbow. First, I thought it was by accident, but then I realised you had intentionally done it."

Daniel became so shy that he covered his face with both palms.

"How silly, Sarah." "You remember all these little incidents?"

"I liked you from the very beginning and wanted to be near you. Even at the time of Holy Communion, which we received, I positioned myself just behind you in the line, so that we could receive Holy Communion together. It was as if we were at the altar of God. " Our Mother Mary united us."

Sarah said it with a sigh of relief and emotion.

Chapter 13

It had been a typical weekend. Seema Chopra and Mary Anthony were on the telephone when the former enquired about Daniel. She had seen news reports on Dubai TV about the accolades he had recently received.

"I am happy that you appreciate Daniel and that I made the right decision in recommending him to your institution."

"Very soon, we are going to invite you too. The management is planning to have an exhibition of Daniel's work at our hotel. It is all in the pipeline at the moment, and we have not informed anyone yet. His Highness and the Sheikha are greatly impressed and appreciate his work."

"Do they like the figurative style of Indian artists?"

"Oh no, Daniel is not doing figurative work. I do not know much about art, but in a broad sense, it is almost like your works, except for the human figures. It's an altogether different style from his earlier works. He works on a large canvas and is heavily influenced by the local landscape and culture, depicting desert dunes, palm trees, and camels in the background. This is the basic tenor and momentum of his paintings. You really must come and see the change in him," Mary explained.

"I am waiting for the right occasion to invite you, not only as a consultant for the development of our school, for which, of course, we greatly admire and appreciate your help."

She also told Seema that Daniel was in great form, and the school management had appreciated him and promoted him as the head of the art department.

"Seemaji, I personally wanted to thank you. His latest venture was to motivate our students between 10 and 15 years of age to participate in an art workshop. All the state dignitaries attended as it was a national event, and His Highness has provided Daniel with every facility to work in our school," Mary said.

"What happy news!" He is as fortunate as one can be successful only through one's own effort and talent. Here, the state hardly gives any of this kind of support to anyone. You know, in our democratic system, they can't promote one individual because it would be considered corruption or nepotism. Here, the story is very different," Seema said.

"Yes, I understand; I lived there for almost twenty-four years. We frequently choose the wrong profession. I enjoyed sports and was a decent basketball player. But I didn't have a choice; I had to take the best job opportunity I could find in order to survive. As you are aware, I am a mother of two and have no dreams for myself. But if I were still there after 35 years, what future would I as an athlete have other than as a last resort, where I would most likely be employed in some government office?"

Mary's tone of voice made it clear that she felt she had missed something in her life. Seema seemed to understand her emotions. Despite the fact that she was only a consultant for their school, she and Mary had become close friends. They would catch up whenever time allowed. Distance was never an issue thanks to Alexander Graham Bell's invention, the telephone. She had the feeling that Mary was not in the mood to end the conversation today. Seema enjoyed chatting as well, and they could talk for hours. It was very different this time. Throughout, the focus remained on Daniel and his work, and Mary did appear to be a big fan of his. Has she fallen in love with him? Oh no! She is also around her own age, 52 to 54, or possibly a few years younger. Seema had met him at the same age. He has a charming personality that is unlike any she has met before—a handsome young man, good-looking, no smoking or drinking, no machismo habits, and yet so talented. There was no other option for her but to ensure he left India.

She used to be possessive of him. Her inner core and professional relationship were more than just friendship and appreciation. There was special bond between them. "Does it go by the name of platonic love?" The answer is either yes or no. Daniel never wanted to be apart from her, and he left with a heavy heart. It was very evident from the way he kissed her and held her gripping her shoulder, that she felt he never wanted to let go. She felt a vacuum, a loneliness, though her husband was very much there. But Daniel was special. She had a deep seated sense that with his departure she had lost something that could never be replaced.

She was aware of her limitations as a painter. She needed to be passionately engaged as a full-time painter after retirement. To stay in the spotlight, which is essential for an artist, she needed a senior artist to help her. Surya fits the bill to, but he will never be able to replace Daniel. Many things happen in life where destiny plays an important role, but in her case, sending him away was entirely her choice.

She was keen on placing him in the right place for her mental satisfaction, so he wouldn't have any regrets about making use of him for her personal gain and popularity. She didn't want him to give her any bad or negative feelings. Besides, she was anxious about the future. There was no guarantee that, after retirement, she could easily avail herself of Daniel's help. The new person in charge might have loaded Daniel with so much work that it might have been difficult for him to paint for her. The last show that Daniel curated received slightly negative reviews. A change was needed for her, not for him. Today, her name features in the art scenario in Delhi. Daniel tried to project her personality, especially through his style of figurative work. He painted only for her to be in the limelight. Her heart always had good wishes and blessings for Daniel.

While Mary on the other end of the line was gushing about Daniel, Seema wondered if she, too, had become obsessed with him. It was certainly possible. Mary, like her, is a mother of two. Life can take unexpected turns in human interactions, no matter your age, society, or social status, while still being committed to family life. Relationships can form quickly and end abruptly. It happens to everyone at least once in their lives. Sometimes, it leads to great happiness but can also end in deep pain and regret. The more Mary spoke of Daniel, Seema got convinced that Mary loved him.

Mary, on the other hand, was making her best efforts to express her gratitude to Seema for her help. "Seemaji, by the way, before I forget, our twins' 13th birthday is falling on August 17. Her Highness is very particular that the birthday be celebrated at her palace. Their younger daughter is one year younger than our twins, and her birthday is also on the same date. I am giving you the invitation much in advance."

"That's so sweet of you, but you know the exam time for pre-board preparation is always in September, and my final year and retirement from the school also end next year in April or May. Trust me, I would love to be there but will not have the time."

"Certainly we will miss you, but very soon we will meet." "The management wants to felicitate you and is waiting for the right occasion, which is the inauguration of our auditorium, now in the finishing stage."

As the two ladies bid each other goodbye, Mary counted her blessings for having Seema as a friend and counsel.

There was not a single time when Mary felt let down about the new school's curriculum development, which she had shared with Seemaji since the beginning. Though Mary assumed responsibility for finance and administration management, she required guidance and technical assistance in all other areas, including staff selection, with Seemaji's input and contribution. All of her advice and support had a human touch to them, which Mary gratefully acknowledged whenever the opportunity arose.

Seemaji is the reason Daniel is at this school today. His was the first name she recommended, despite the fact that art was the last priority. Mary had no idea why Daniel's name was in the spotlight. She adores him without a doubt. Seema's voice has a special sweetness whenever his name is mentioned in conversation.

Chapter 13

Daniel and Sarah make an attractive couple. Whenever Mary sits alone at her desk after her hectic, busy schedule, the forgotten memories flash back to her.

"If only I had remained a single mother and dared to make the difficult decision to keep the infant with my parents at first!"

Was it a fair decision? Then her beloved mother persuaded her, 'Look, you're only 22 years old; don't make an emotional decision.' You know the child's father will never recognise him, and he may even refuse to accept him, and you are adamant about not telling his family. The child will be labelled a bastard, a child born outside of marriage. It is a harsh reality that he will have to live a shameful life. Our society has not matured to the point of accepting the 'single mother' status. It's still a Western concept.

"Mary, I am your mother; I can feel your agony. Let us think for the time being that we keep the baby; what about you? You are too young, and for any marriage proposal, a woman who has no chastity will always be in question. All your life, you will have to face the shame, including for us. You cannot ignore, when born into a good family that no bad name should be brought upon the parents and the society we belong to. The only option in front of us is to leave the child in a safe place and in safe hands," her mother convinced her.

During that difficult time, she never imagined the consequences of her action or that she might never get to see him again. Even today, her heart weeps whenever she thinks about him. She never wanted to be this cruel. She was happy when he was growing in her womb. She took the utmost care all through her pregnancy period to be well nourished, read all the children's books, even avoided night duty, and did not see sad or horror movies during that period until the delivery date.

Her mother had not planned at that time what was to be done when the child was born. She convinced Mary not to try and read the child's future while it was in the womb. "He will bring his own destiny and luck.

Let the child be born, and both of you are safe. After the delivery, we will make the decision."

Her mother initially planned on taking the child to her native village, but after speaking to her husband, the plan was changed. He said that the consequences would be awful and that the entire family's happiness and peace would be shattered. Not a day has gone by that I haven't thought of him. Her mother said he was like her father, having big legs and hands, and that his eyes and nose are similar to hers, with the exception of his colour. He'll grow up to be quite tall, as Mama predicted. He was a contented infant during those three days of his infancy at the hospital and the subsequent three days at home; he never disturbed her sleep even once. She recalled how her breasts were always overflowing with milk, soaking her bra and top. She wanted to give him all of her milk to last for the rest of his life because those were tense days when every moment counted.

She had not revealed to any of her friends that she was pregnant. She took a three-month break from the hospital, citing her father's illness as the justification. Her mother believed that relationships that resulted in pregnancy could never be kept a secret, so she went to Delhi. Her mother lived with her in Delhi for three months.

Her heart wanted to catch a fleeting glimpse of her handsome child, wherever he might be. She had terrible nights after giving him up. She would awaken to find her pillow soaked with tears and her sheets covered in breast milk. She desired to leave her current situation and have absolutely no memory of it for the rest of her life.

She made the difficult decision to leave India on the day her hospital bond expired. She was certain that if she stayed back, she, would experience a collapse since she was unable to carry the weight on her heart. Because she had no time for daydreaming due to her busy schedule, she forgot how quickly time passed.

Paramedical workers were in limited supply all across the world during that time, especially in Europe, the Americas, and the Middle East. She chose to travel to Dubai because it required less time to obtain a visa than other locations. The trip with the Delhi staffing agency went without a hitch. She had three years of nursing experience after graduating. Since the hospital did not want to offer family accommodations or maternity leave, the agency preferred single, unmarried women.

At the time, a virginity test was not required to travel to Dubai, which was fortunate for her because she had the heart of a mother and the body of a married woman. As a result, at the age of 23, she arrived in Dubai and began working at Abdul Al Rashid Hospital. It almost took six years of hard work to reach the position of matron in the hospital.

The first time she was on vacation, she chose to travel through Delhi because she wanted to visit the MC Sisters Ashram. The whole idea was to get a chance to see him. Maybe just a glance—how he looks and how much he has grown. She had been dreaming of meeting her "little one" and counting down the days until it would happen.

The Sisters treat all children equally and similarly, and none is granted a special advantage unless they are unwell or have a disability. Mary's main purpose was to see her child, but there were no rules for giving special privileges to visitors unless there was a solid reason, like adoption or parental identity. She knew her limitations in the first place when they left the child; they had not even bothered to wait, acknowledge, or see the sister in charge. Today, under what pretext can she get entry to the Ashram except as a visitor like any other who comes to give them a donation or gift as charity?

This was his third year, and she was on holiday for Christmas. She purchased dresses for many children, ranging in age from three to four years. Sister Susan introduced her to the residents as Mary who was a former student of St. Stephens Hospital and working in Dubai she is now on her annual leave.

The Sisters were happy, and as part of their hospitality, which is a custom they extend to every visitor, invited her to join them for tea. Mary was overjoyed to stay longer on the premises and spend time with them.

She asked politely about the kids' future and their education. The Sisters responded in a very sincere and honest manner. The kids are transferred to various Catholic mission orphanages after they turn 10 years old. The girls typically travel to St. Antony's in Bangalore or a place maintained by the SD Sisters in Meerut. Everything will be based on available seats. In Lucknow, The Gabriel Brothers operate a centre for boys.

The MC Sisters also claimed that when couples come for adoption, certain children, mainly females, are extremely fortunate. Mary was relieved to learn that girls are favoured. She was relieved that her child would have a very remote chance of travelling overseas to someone's house and would be raised in Lucknow by the Gabriel Brothers.

As the time passed, she realised the chance to see her child was rare, and any attempt to recognise him would also bring unwanted suspicion. Even the Sisters have no authority in their jurisdiction to entertain visitors without solid reasons written into the law. As it may bring unwanted false claims, the visitors must produce legal documents of authority for the purpose of their visit. No one is permitted to spend more than the stipulated time.

She realised that staying on campus for an extended period of time was not worth it. She was only thinking about how to compensate for the guilt she had caused and was looking for an opportunity, leaving no doubt about the reason for her visit. Giving her conscience peace was important to her, so she looked for methods to compensate in some way without revealing her identity.

Sister Susan asked as she was leaving the Ashram, "Whenever you are in Delhi, please do drop in and remember us in your prayers." She thanked her and asked for Sister Susan's phone number. She took some photos with her, assuring Sister that she would be in touch with them. "Sister, I need your blessings and prayers, as I will be leaving for Dubai by the first week of January," she said.

"Praise the Lord, Mary; next time we wish to see you not alone." Sister Susan was humorous, and in a short time they had become friends.

"Sure, Sister, not immediately, but it is all in God's hands, and He has a plan for me."

"Yes, we will pray, and all the best wishes to you, Mary."

They said goodbye to each other, and she left the campus. It was not fair to linger, and she did not want to give anyone a chance to doubt her intentions. All through, her eyes were on the search for him, thinking he may appear from somewhere at any time and hoping against hope for a glance.

Since then, she has made it a habit to visit an orphanage every year on December 23rd, bringing gifts for the unfortunate children who have been deprived of parental love and mother's care. She imagined that many other mothers, like her, had gone through a similar ordeal.

Meanwhile, she received many different marriage proposals. She got to meet a lot of Malayalis who were patients and employees at the Dubai hospital. She made the firm decision that she would not fall in love with anyone before marriage. The Malayali community celebrated Onam and Christmas with get-togethers and cultural programmes. She had no time to participate in any activities aside from attending the programme. There was no time for socialising between the hospital, the patients, and the hostel. She chose to stay at the hospital hostel because she enjoyed the atmosphere and was well-liked by the staff.

Mr. Antony Sir was the engineer-in-charge of their hospital's construction work. He was already employed by the Trust that ran the hospital. She had seen him, when he would come to enquire about the welfare of construction staff in the casualty ward. She found him to be a very patient and compassionate man. They would exchange pleasantries when they met. When they met for the first time, he casually asked her the name of her village and her parents' names. He was addressed as 'Antony Sir' by all on the campus. She considered him to be a mature man based on his appearance and behaviour. She couldn't recall if they had ever discussed her or his marital status. He was the point of contact for any civil maintenance issues in their hostel or hospital.

The day Mary was promoted to Matron, the hospital staff arranged a celebration in the hospital cafeteria. All hospital personnel, including service and maintenance personnel, were present, as was Antony Sir. After cutting the cake, everyone congratulated her, and he also came forward and handed her a small bouquet of roses. When she returned home with all of her gifts, she noticed Anthony Sir's flower bouquet had only three flowers, and they were all different colours: white, red, and pink. It carried a small card that read: "All best wishes; we are both from the same village. Until the fifth class, your mother was my primary school teacher. With love, Antony." 'With love'? Instead of 'With regards' or "Good wishes"?

Mary was puzzled yet tickled nonetheless. In the last five years, they had met many times, but not even once had he expressed any special interest or enthusiasm in being friends with her. Now, why had he written "With love"? She kept the card inside her diary because something felt special about the message. She smiled, thinking he had taken five years to spell "with love," but it was possible he had written it in a light-hearted mood or on the spur of the moment.

When I see him again, I'll ask what year he graduated and in which he was in my mother's class? Her mother will be overjoyed to learn that one of her students, who is also from the same village, works in the same company as her daughter in a senior position.

She found it amusing that she could have known him a little sooner! What is going to be the difference? Is he really saying "love," or is she imagining or taking the words too seriously? Wait and see. He will undoubtedly observe her facial expression the next time they meet. She can express herself in three ways: seriously, as usual, or casually.

She can start by telling him that she relayed his information to Mummy and enquired about his parents and family name. She was certain her mother would enquire about his pet name, his parents' names, and his age. That was her usual method of determining whether he was a good match for her.

She kept all three flowers, but a thought occurred to her: "Why three?" Her thirty-first birthday was the day before the function. He may have heard from her colleagues and become aware of it, so he sent three flowers, each in a different colour, and he did so very diligently. He does have a sense of humour, and it was thoughtful of him, knowing she is his primary schoolteacher Anna's daughter. But until yesterday, he had never taken her name!

When she tried to sleep after dinner, Anthony Sir's thoughts kept her awake. She had met him on official business a number of times. Why had she never considered him as a potential partner or husband? She assumed he was married because he looked quite mature. May she have disliked him?

He was handsome but not romantic or articulate. He was always to the point. Is he the same way about everything—not timid but also not an extrovert? He was good at explaining everything in detail to the staff and was very prompt in responding to their complaints.

How does she know he isn't married or engaged? If he is, why did he sign "with love"? She has been on campus for six years, and if he were married, she would have met his wife. However, he has never brought his wife or children with him on any occasion. "Why are you breaking your head, Mary?" He could be married for all you know; it is not required that the spouses of all married men and women reside in Dubai. Sixty percent of Keralites are content with sending monthly remittances and taking one month of annual leave. Obtaining a work visa is extremely difficult unless you are a paramedic or technically qualified.

She had decided to call her mother in the evening because she would be waiting for her call to find out about her promotion celebrations. After her graduation, when she was 21 years old, there was a big celebration at her home with her parents, her elder sister, her husband, and her cousins. How the years had passed! Nine years had passed. She has been through motherhood, separation, and then leaving the country on a long journey to relocate in a distant land, only to go away from her past.

But thankfully, sleep did not evade her. She still remembered how she jumped out of bed when the phone's sharp ring woke her. Her parents had been worried because she had not called home earlier in the evening, as was expected of her.

"Are you okay, baby? You didn't call yesterday." Her mother's anxious tone had greeted her. She had given them an exhaustive account of how her birthday and promotion celebration went. She had been checking on her father's diabetes readings as part of her routine since she left home. In those days, her parents' home in the village was being extended, and Mary, as the dutiful daughter, was chipping in with as much funding as she could manage. And just when she least expected it, her mother popped the question about Anthony Sir.

"Little one, pay attention, please. Do you know anybody by the name Anthony George?" When she said yes in the most casual voice she could muster, a volley of questions, from how long to what she thinks of him and what he does, were thrown at her. Her answer that she had known him for a considerable period of time resulted in some teasing by her parents.

She was informed that Anthony Sir had told his parents that he liked her, and his parents in turn had approached hers with a proposal for marriage. Her parents were obviously delighted at the prospect of her getting married. But Mary, a little embarrassed, quickly hung up after promising to make up her mind within a week. "Mummy, give me a week; I will call you back. Let me make up my mind. Bye, Mummy, I love you and Papa." She had disconnected the call before they could ask anything else.

The present development had turned all her plans on their heads. Now, where to start? To begin the topic, she had planned to tell Anthony Sir that she had spoken to her mother and she enquired about him and the year when he was in her class. But now everything had been turned upside down. If he opens the topic, then all will be fine.

If he doesn't initiate the topic, then what? As a courtesy, she will have to say she spoke to Mummy, she remembers you. Should she say our parents met and spoke about us, and they are proposing that we get married? After much mental back and forth, she finally decided to speak up as appropriate for the circumstances.

They are both on the same campus and have already had several encounters, but he has yet to initiate or express any attempts to start a friendship-related conversation. He may be a little orthodox, cautious, and not outgoing.

Nonetheless, she would have to wait as he made the effort to approach his parents about the idea. She made up her mind that if he enquires about her during their upcoming meeting regarding any past relationships or indiscretions, she won't lie and live with guilt for the rest of her life.

The following day, she went to the hospital cafeteria during the evening tea break. She sat at an empty table, opened her notepad, and began to write. She pretended to be waiting for someone when she did not actually order tea and snacks. She figured that if Anthony Sir was serious about her, he would walk in to find out her reaction to his interesting bouquet that was marked "With Love." It had hardly been five minutes when she heard someone approaching. She purposely didn't look up and continued to write.

"Hi Mary, can I sit?" It was Anthony Sir. "How are you? Did your parents call you? I love to be frank and honest. I told my mother last week about you, and my father told me today that they met your parents," he said in one breath as he pulled out a chair.

Mary smiled, stopped writing, and gave full attention to what he was saying.

"Mummy spoke to me, and I said give me a little time because in the last five years, even though we have met frequently, neither of us has ever directly or indirectly stated a desire for marriage or a romantic relationship, so I thought we would meet first,» I said.

"That is true. I had personal reasons. During this period, my two sisters got married. Once I got married, I didn't want to hear from my wife how she had to share my family's responsibilities. I felt it was my moral duty, and I did it for my satisfaction."

"I greatly appreciate that. Sometimes, I do feel the absence of a brother. By the way, if you don't mind, when did you decide or feel that I could be your life partner?"

"I am not sure of the exact time or date. But I must confess, though, that the first time you went on leave, I asked your friend if you had gone to get married. I was very happy with the answer I got. She said, she didn't think you had immediate plans for marriage. I learned you had gone on your annual vacation. God willing, I can make a proposal when the time comes. So that's what happened."

"Is there anything special about me?" Mary asked.

"First, I have never seen you in any man's company in a public place. Your straight-forward manner and steady walk made me feel we could get along well together."

"Thanks. I'm thirty years old. I've been residing outside the state for about ten years. All questions you have about me must be asked. I don't want to learn in the future that you never considered or felt this. You are free to ask me anything at this point."

"That's an honest answer, Mary, and it's exactly what I intended to tell you. I too have a history of school, college, a service term, and some loves and dislikes. I never proposed to anyone or had an argument with anyone. I was convinced that I wouldn't marry until I was thirty or thirty-two years old. And eventually, when I marry, there is no guarantee that person will be perfect. But this is no compromise either. That is, in a nutshell, the truth. I am living in the present and planning for the future; the past has passed me by with no questions asked. I'm glad that instead of racing to escape the guilt of my shortcomings, I'm enjoying today and looking forward to having a family life," Anthony Sir stated.

"Now, don't ask me any questions; don't lie on principle. So, you and I agree on this?" Mary asked.

He stood up, approached her, and hugged and kissed her on both cheeks. She purposefully held his palm for a few moments, a clear, honest touch of understanding. There were no words or expressions.

At last he asked, "Coffee or tea?"

"What do you like?"

He said, "Tea." To date, that has been their preference. That was all there was to their engagement.

Except for one minor blip, life would have been as smooth as butter. Despite their good health, Mary and her husband were unable to conceive. She began blaming herself. She thought she was being punished by God for abandoning her baby. What if she had decided to keep her son? Today, she might be a single mother with a 27-year-old grown-up son or even a grandmother. Who knows who would have accepted her, who would have questioned her chastity, and who would have ended their relationship with her on moral grounds?

Anthony had given up hope and was on the verge of adopting a child. But they realised just in time that they were faced with an andrological issue. Testing revealed that her husband, despite being a highly healthy and active man, had a low sperm count. At the age of forty-two, Mary experienced motherhood once more thanks to medical advancements. God was once again kind. By gifting her twins, he made up for lost time.

Her twins, Aryan and Ananya, were born on August 17, bringing good tidings into their lives. Their birthday fell on the same day as the Malayalam New Year. As per the Malayalam calendar, they were born on the first day of the first month of Chingam. Their birth brought peace and happiness on many levels. Not only were the parents thrilled with their bundles of joy, but the grandparents' long wait for grandchildren was also over. Mary's mother, who had been burdened with guilt for advising her to give up her first child, could finally breathe easily.

Whenever they called, Mary's mother would always inadvertently end up talking about when Mary would conceive. And once it was clear that Anthony's health was the cause of the delay, conversations would end with asking if he was taking his medicines regularly. She is simply thankful for all God has given her.

She remembers how hectic the days were when the school was being set up. She was so thankful to the Lord for having sent Daniel and Sarah. Daniel was the first staff member to arrive. Though he was very young, he was considered the senior most as he had joined duty first. The young couple was literally God sent because of the way they had helped relieve her of her many burdens. Without being asked, they had simply pitched in with organising and receiving the staff from the airport and helping them settle down.

Though Daniel's wife, Sarah, was not a faculty member or officially holding any position, she took it upon herself to help the new faculty even though she was herself new to the country. No one asked them or delegated any particular duty, but they still did their best whenever there was an opportunity. The service they rendered was significant and done with the utmost integrity at the time of the school's establishment, and the management accepted and noticed it. Later, whenever the opportunity arose, the faculty repeatedly stated that they admired both, particularly Sarah.

When Mary called to invite Sarah and Daniel to her home on Aryan and Ananya's birthday, August 17, Sarah asked if she could help with the party planning.

"Ma'am, I have a lot of spare time." We had all kinds of feasts and celebrations at the convent. "I can assist you in decorating and making all necessary arrangements," Sarah said. Mary was overjoyed with the young girl's assistance. It appeared to be an unassuming gesture, but she has always felt that when both of them addressed her as "Ma'am," the last 'm' is always silent, and it sounds to her as "Ma," and perhaps they prefer to call her Ma. She is aware that they are both orphans, and it tugs at her heart. Since then, it has been their privilege to do all of the decorations and arrangements for birthdays, Christmas, and New Year's, as well as any other gatherings they have at Mary's house.

Not only Mary but also her husband, Anthony Sir, enjoy their company, particularly Sarah's. He makes her laugh, cracks jokes with her, and enquires about her convent life and childhood. She explained everything to him as someone who was very close to her. Almost seven years have passed, and their friendship has grown to the point where he treats her as if she were a daughter or a younger sister. He makes it a point to bring Sarah home at the end of each month. She prepares all Kerala dishes, for which she was trained at the Malayali Sisters convent. They were able to connect quickly and enjoyed each other's company. Sarah became intimately familiar with the children as well, and the entire family believes she is a member of the family rather than an outsider. Mary enjoyed Sarah's presence and felt she was a gift, and after many long years of her life, there was someone there to share her burden of household duties on all occasions, and she silently enjoyed their presence in her heart.

Sarah had quickly become a big sister by talking to the kids and paying frequent visits. Aryan and Ananya were very comfortable with Sarah whenever Mary and Anthony went on short vacations or official trips, and it had gotten to the point where the children never felt they missed their parents. Daniel was gentle and polite, a serious man who was not particularly outspoken. Meanwhile, Sarah grew so close to Mary that they began sharing all family matters, and there was no incident that they had not shared with each other.

Sarah told her, "Ma'am, I know where my mother is and where she came from." She disliked making any effort to locate her parents. "Allow them to be happy wherever they are". She came to ask one of her MC Sisters. Her mother's name is Rose Gauda, and she currently resides in the United States. She had a nursing background as well. Because of her financial situation at the time of her birth, she had no choice, and she was also unmarried, as the Sisters informed her.

"You have been married for seven to eight years; when do you plan to start a family and have children?" Mary had recently enquired out of love. Though it is personal, as a woman, I can tell you that the longer you wait, the more complications will arise when you do want to have children. Consider it motherly advice."

"We do want to start a family, Ma." We both enjoy children, but for various reasons, we have put it off. We had almost forgotten about it after we moved here and because of our friendships with Aryan and Ananya. Now there will be no more delays; Daniel is also mentally prepared."

One day, Mary, unable to help herself, asked if, as orphans, Sarah or Daniel had ever faced abuse of any kind. "Do you ever discuss with each other your childhood, your life in the convent, and his at Gabriel Brothers? Were there any sad incidents or abuses that you faced that you never wanted to discuss or reveal? This sort of incident sometimes haunts you, and there will be trauma about starting a family or parenthood. Does he ever tell you anything about his parents, who they may be?"

"Ma, it is very touching that you have asked these questions. Sincerely, because of the Sisters' care and affection, I never missed not having parents. Maybe it is one of the reasons why I have never bothered about my parents. But I confess he is very possessive about his mother; he feels he knows her. With great difficulty and my prayers, he left Delhi. For him, Seema Ma'am was his world and everything. She loved me so much, but I felt insecure sometimes. Though he never told me as his wife anything about her, I can make out that Seema Ma'am had a special place in his life. For him, she was his mother, friend, and mentor, and on some occasions we used to fight and argue." Sarah had continued: "If he had not been given the baptismal name Mario, it was Ashok Mario Daniel. He always says that one day he will find out who his real mother is. He worships her in his heart. He always says she is a saint and very much wanted him to be born; he is very firm in his belief," Sarah continued.

It was as if someone on the inside had stopped her from asking for any more information, whether from her or Daniel. A healed-up wound should not be scratched, regardless of the outcome, even if the truth is revealed or he finds his mother. They can feel, admire, and love from afar, which is possible in any case. Allow the hidden beauty of love to remain and bask in the glory of dreams. Time is the best healer of old wounds.

Daniel had become the ultimate world for Aryan and Ananya because their parents were too busy with their professional lives to devote much time to their company. They had started asking Daniel before choosing their clothes, costumes, and even books to read. Despite their parents' love and luxury, their children found something special in Daniel and Sarah. They treat and speak to them as if they were their elder brother and sister, irrespective to the age difference. It is more than just sibling love.

Antony Sir would scold Aryan and Ananya and tell them to behave, but Daniel and Sarah would interject and stop him. "They enjoy our company, and we enjoy theirs. Where does the question of respect and age arise when they love us and we too have a good time with them?" Daniel had asked.

"Dad, please. If *Achachen* and *Chechy* have no problem, then what is the big issue?" The twins had chimed in unison.

Mary, on her part, would warn Daniel and Sarah against giving unbridled freedom to her kids. "Tomorrow, don't make any complaint to me that they are not giving you due respect."

She decided to let this relationship continue as it was so that there would be no more debate or inquisitiveness about either of them. Her husband warned Mary not to enquire further about Sarah and Daniel in their casual conversations at home because it would not bring her happiness. Antony Sir advised Mary to refrain from asking because they may have no idea about their lineage, and it could hurt their feelings and play with their emotions. Following that, Mary took a different path, realising that if conversations between individuals do not bring benefits or happiness, it is best to discontinue them.

Daniel and Sarah's intimacy with her children and her husband had unknowingly built into a strong bond that she could not define in words. A sense of loneliness had seeped into her after she left her village. She had felt that her relatives, other than her parents, had become distant. But after Daniel and Sarah came into their lives, the heartache slowly disappeared. Anthony was like the Rock of Gibraltar. All these years, outside of her immediate family, she could not count anyone as her own. But now that void has been filled. She knew Daniel and Sarah were there for her and her family.

"Daniel will be the guardian angel of Aryan and Ananya." This thought struck her a number of times, but other than her mother, she could not share it with anyone. Her mother, too, had not objected but assured her.

"God has plans; now why do you worry? He sent someone to you; what more do you want?"

"Mama, earlier, when he came to meet me for the first time, I forgot to tell you about his presence in the school. I felt he was my lost son. I can feel like someone is saying to me without words, from his expression and body language, 'Don't worry, I am here,'. I can't put it into words, but I can sense it. That is his attitude. But while there are men and ladies, senior and superior to him, who are all faithful and loyal, Daniel is an exception. He gets involved in everything without talking about it, but none of his colleagues have ever expressed that he is interfering or overbearing. How to explain his particular temperament?" Mary asked her mother.

Her mother had not rebuffed her but only attested to her belief. "I can understand, darling; your Papa is of the same nature. You can take it as an attitude, and it is all in the genes."

However, when she previously told her mother about Daniel, who was also raised at the MC Sister's centre in Delhi, her mother ignored her. Maybe she doesn't want to hurt Mary, or maybe she doesn't want old memories to haunt her, or maybe she just doesn't want her to be miserable. Mothers are usually loving, but when it comes to their children, they are extremely selfish.

The auditorium will be completed in less than a year. She was looking forward to it with bated breath. She and her employers, Sheikh Abdul Al Rashid and Sheikha Nabeesa, were the only ones who knew what a wonderful surprise it held. How much joy it would provide to everyone.

Chapter 14

The big day had come. It was a major day not only for the school but also for Mary and Daniel on a personal level. It was Christmas Eve, but more importantly, the brand new auditorium was going to be inaugurated during the school's annual function. It was going to be a significant event for the city. Newspapers and TV networks from all over the UAE were vying to cover the ceremony. The list of invited guests and dignitaries who would be in attendance read like a who's who of the city. The management team of the Abdul Al Rashid Trust, under the direction of His Highness Sheikh Abdul Al Rashid and Sheikha, had ensured every i had been dotted and t crossed. The school's and the Trust's prestige were at stake, and everything was meticulously planned. Mary Antony and her team had spent the previous week going through everything with a fine tooth comb.

The heads of each department were kept informed. Everyone agreed that Daniel should be a part of the organising committee and given responsibility for a crucial area. When Mary informed him of her decision, he respectfully declined. He said that he didn't want the range of his work to be constrained. "I can do much better without being part of the committee. If I am delegated to one particular assignment, then I have to be content with it. My total involvement will be there for 24 hours, and I am happy to help out in every way." Mary had smiled and accepted his decision because he was correct. He was such a powerhouse of talent and energy. If he were given just one portfolio, it would be like putting him in a strait jacket.

How can one not admire him with that personality and attitude? Whenever he came to discuss any difficult issue with Mary, she ended up agreeing with him because he did not come with problems but with solutions and only needed her seal of approval. She became his silent soul whenever she was with him. She loved hearing his voice and occasionally, even without reason, used to invite him to her cabin. She noted that he would sometimes appear with or without a serious subject, and she knew he just wanted to be with her.

About a year ago, he came to her with a proposal for a painting that would be a gift to the school. The only catch was that it would be done in complete secrecy.

"I am seriously working on a large canvas. I need to finish it in complete privacy. Only you can come and see. No one else will be allowed. I want to unveil this painting on inauguration day. The full size of the stage will be our backdrop. Curtains will be drawn throughout the entire programme. Ma, I need a yes from you. And if you like the idea, then it will be a total surprise to all. Of course, except you."

She was so taken by the proposition that there was no way she could object. This was what made him so unique. Whenever he said something or came up with an idea, it was always backed by sound reasoning. He never left room for any criticism. Yet, he was never egoistic. Always humble and direct.

While giving him her approval, she advised him to keep it a secret from her as well. She had asked whether he needed any financial support for the project. His response made her heart swell with pride and her eyes well up.

"No, Ma, this will be a gift and an asset to our school. And will always be remembered as a shared contribution, especially because of the opportunity given by you to Sarah and me."

"Our, you mean?"

"Yes, Ma, it will be our contribution." He had replied with an emphasis on 'our'.

She understood the meaning of 'our'. She turned her head away from him, unable to stop the tears that ran down her cheeks.

He immediately rushed to her. Without any reservation, he came and stood behind her, then put his hands on her shoulders. It felt like she had been waiting for a long time for this. She lacked words to express how she felt, but she sensed his inner strength. As he bowed and lightly wiped her tears, her left hand caressed his head. It was all so spontaneous.

His action was against office policy and decorum, but both were on a planet of their own. "Thanks, dear, I am so overwhelmed with emotion. When you said, 'ours', I couldn't control myself."

There had been emotional moments in the past, but they were never definitive. They had formed an unspoken bond, and it was so strong that everyone in the Anthony family enjoyed their proximity.

When he and Sarah addressed her as "Ma'am", the last 'm' was always silent. It warmed her heart to hear them call her Ma. Maybe they meant she was their mother. It was a word she adored. She felt loved and fulfilled. Life was treating her well, and she was enjoying every moment of it.

It was also the school's seventh anniversary. Everyone was overjoyed, including the founders. A new school block had been built for the students who would be progressing to high school. Moreover, the new auditorium, with its 800-seat capacity, set a new record among schools. It was to be dedicated to the founders, His Highness Sheikh Abdul Al Rashid and his wife.

To give it an international flavour, organisers decided that all students would dress in their ethnic attire while the teachers would don the national costume. Besides, there was to be no professional master of ceremonies; instead, the head girl and head boy would host and anchor the function. The idea was to showcase how the faculty had trained their students to assume positions of leadership and built their self-confidence. Aside from the cultural programmes, the organising committee had planned a number of surprises for the event. The fact that the institution had grown and expanded so much in just seven years was a matter of pride for all.

As the Sheikh of Dubai cut the ribbon and inaugurated the auditorium, thunderous claps reverberated around the hall as flash lights went off from all corners. Mary was getting goose bumps. As she sat there with the Sheikha on one side and special guest Seemaji on the other, tears sprung up, blurring her vision. She was almost choking with emotion and was so glad that she had decided not to be the anchor today. Besides, her dear Kameela, Sheikh Abdul Al Rashid's daughter, and her own son Aryan were doing a fabulous job emceeing it as if they were born for it.

As the last of the dance shows by a group of middle schoolers ended, it was a signal for Mary that the two-hour function was coming to an end. Everything, from the various cultural shows to the prize-giving ceremony, had gone off without a hitch. Cheers and applause greeted every aspect of the performances that had been staged. It was clear from the response that the audience was enthralled by the events of the evening. Now was the time for surprises. She knew there were going to be two of them.

The first of the surprises was for Seema Chopra. Second, there was supposed to be an unveiling of Daniel's painting. On behalf of the school and the trust, the head boy acknowledged the DIS principal's contribution to their school. It was a rather emotional moment, as both ladies were visibly moved when Seema Chopra accepted her memento from none other than her friend Mary Anthony. As they were about to leave the stage, the head girl announced she had a second surprise in store for the evening. When the Sheikh and the Sheikha were invited on stage to "felicitate Mary Anthony, Ma'am", Mary was totally stunned. The surprise was on her! As she received her gold shield, the whole auditorium rose to their feet to give her a standing ovation.

Her voice trembled with emotion as she thanked His Highness and his wife, Mrs. Nabeesa Sheikh, for the trust they had placed in her, and she also expressed her gratitude for the moral support, particularly from the faculty and parents. "Respectable Hon. Minister, Your Highness and Mrs. Nabeesa Sheikh, and all faculty members and parents, this is an opportunity for me to express my eternal gratitude to God and the founders who contributed to the growth of this institution from a play school to the 7th standard, a long journey. You may have experienced anxiety as parents, wondering where your children will go after the 7th.

However, His Highness and family had planned ahead of time, and the new building is now ready to take all of your children to higher classes comparable to any international standard."

On behalf of all parents, she went to thank the management for their wholehearted effort. She went on to express her gratitude to Seema Chopra "for her help and wisdom in establishing this school, especially in the selection of the faculty". She concluded that it was a wonderful opportunity to recognise everyone in the faculty, including students and parents.

To everyone's surprise, when they thought the function was over, Kameela and Aryan announced in tandem that the surprises for the evening were not over yet. "You may be wondering who the Golden Shield on the stage is waiting for." Mary and Seema were requested to unveil the white curtain covering the backdrop.

As the curtains moved to the sides, hushed silence filled the place as everyone sat captivated by the image that emerged. It was a life-size painting. A scene so tranquil of the morning sun settling down over the sand dunes, with little plants and droplets in the background; in the mid-ground, a realistic scene of the capital city; and in the foreground, a woman sitting on a donkey, carrying her infant in her lap, and a man walking behind. The figures were like shadows in semi-abstract form.

It was a symbolic representation of the Virgin Mary with the Infant Jesus, or simply "a mother and child." However, the artist had left it to the viewer's imagination, despite the fact that the woman was the only figure prominently featured. As the audience marvelled at the painting's beauty, Seema Chopra was asked to say a few words about art teacher Daniel, who the head girl revealed was the painter.

After Seema spoke about Daniel and how proud he had made her by proving he was one of the best artists in his sphere, it was Mary's turn.

"I will fail in my duty if I do not recognise Mr. Daniel, the great artist who has brought fame and glory to the school today. The entire state is talking about him, and the school is known for mentioning his name wherever we go," she stated.

The two young emcees then requested that all those present on the dais, including their Highnesses and Mary and Seema Chopra, hand over the trophy to Daniel.

Daniel gracefully moved up to the platform after rising from the floor and turning to face every invitee with his hands folded. The entire audience began to applaud and support him. His Highness and the Sheikha stood on either side of the Hon. Minister in the centre, while Madam Seema and Mary stood next to each other and clapped their hands. Along with his wife, the Hon. Minister, His Highness, presented the souvenir to Daniel.

Once more, cameras were frantically clicking away to record the moment, lighting up the entire auditorium. With the large painting in the backdrop, it was a lovely scene to see. The microphone was given to Daniel as the dignitaries sat down. He requested Mary and Seema to stay by his side as he took the microphone, and since the microphone was on, everyone could hear him.

"It took me nearly a year to complete the painting. I dedicate it to all mothers and children, as well as the Mothers of Charity who raised me as an infant. His tone was distinctly husky. "Today, on New Year's Eve, I'd like to say that I'm not sure whether my birthday is on the 23rd or the 24th because I was six or seven days old when I was left at the door of Mothers of Charity. When I was 10 years old, the MC Sisters sent me to the Gabriel Brothers, who raised me." There was total silence as he spoke.

"First, I salute my mother, who gave me birth without fear or shame, who stood up to all the pain and humiliation, and without whom I would not be here today." I'd like to thank Brother Vincent of the Gabriel Brothers School for being my mentor and guide during my school days, as well as Seema Ma'am for giving me a chance at her prestigious school and later recommending me to this great institution. I am honoured and grateful once more, Ma'am.

I'd like to thank Mary Ma for believing in my abilities and promoting me for the past seven years to do something in the field of art and to explore my field as an artist." Thank you very much, Hon. Minister, Your Highness, and Ma'am. I'm here because of your generosity. Today, as previously stated, is my birthday, which I doubt because I don't know the exact date of my birth. My birthday is December 24th, according to school records, but only my mother knows."

"Mr. Daniel's birthday is on December 23rd," Mary, who was on his right side, interrupted. Despite the fact that she had not taken the microphone in her hand, her voice was audible to the audience. All of the students and invitees were moved by her words, and many were wiping away tears. It was a very touching moment, and Mary confirmed once more, "According to the school records, Mr. Daniel's birthday is on December 23rd, 1980." Her voice was hoarse with controlled tears.

Daniel stood silent for a moment. Finally, after what seemed like an eternity, he regained his voice and continued. "I am here because of Seemaji and her generous help to establish me at the beginning of my career."

Seema Chopra reached up, covered his mouth, and took the microphone away from him, much to everyone's surprise. "I have no shame today in revealing the truth without bias; he is Daniel, who has established himself as a towering figure among students, teachers, and the art world. I became an artist because of him, not the other way around." Seemaji's hands trembled, and tears streamed down her cheeks.

Mary quickly moved between Daniel and Seema, wrapping her arms around them. As the National Anthem was played, the audience fell silent.

As the dignitaries left the stage, the Hon. Minister approached Daniel and shook his hand. "The state will confer honorary citizenship on you and commission you for an installation in the state palace. I am very impressed to see the large canvas on the stage," he said, patting Daniel on the shoulder.

Daniel kneeled in front of the King and the Hon. Minister as a sign of humility. Mary came near Daniel, lifted him up, and took his hand in a firm grip. As they exited the stage, they walked side by side, heads held high. Both wore an air of free abandon.

"Daniel, do you still miss your mother?"

It was the voice of his unknown mother.

"No M'am"…

Printed in the USA
CPSIA information can be obtained
at www.ICGtesting.com
LVHW091156071124
795951LV00001B/22